# A Surcease of Sorrow

Andy C Wareing

ISBN- 9798514050383

Cover design by: Andy C Wareing
Cover Photo by Eyasu Etsub on Unsplash

Printed in the United States of America

andycwareing@gmail.com
https://pandaproofed.wordpress.com

## *Dedication*

Dedicated to Paula, my beautiful wife and best friend.

*Contents*

# *Chapter I*

*Once upon a midnight dreary, while I pondered, weak and weary, over many a quaint and curious volume of forgotten lore.*
*While I nodded, nearly napping, suddenly there came a tapping...*

Three o'clock in the morning found me running through the deserted streets carrying only my cane and brown leather medical bag. The rain swept in curtains across the shiny cobbles, reflected the faint moonlight that peeked at intervals between heavy clouds. The wind from the harbor screeched, October cold, between the buildings of downtown. The gas lamps guided my journey; flickered luminance threw verdurous creeping shadows across the alleyways and shuttered glass frontages of the stores on High Street. My mentor and friend of the last twenty years lay in distress in the parlor of Gunners, a tavern on East Lombard Street, in Baltimore's seventh ward.

I had been wakened only thirty minutes earlier by a

frenzied banging on my door. A small shabby boy stood in the shadows of the stoop holding a penned note that summoned my presence to the inn. The note was addressed to me, Doctor J. E. Snodgrass and read:

*"Dear Doctor Snodgrass, there is a gentleman, rather the worse for wear, at Gunners who goes under the cognomen of Edgar, and who appears in great distress, & he says he is acquainted with you, and I assure you, he is in need of immediate assistance."*

Edgar had been found only two hours prior, by the author of the note, a certain William W. Walker. Mr. Walker had found Edgar by chance, lying in the street outside the tavern, soaked, shivering and largely incoherent. Edgar was a stranger to him but thinking him a helpless drunk, and the weather being brutal, had taken pity and helped him into the sanctuary and shelter of the tavern to recover. Between his ramblings, Edgar had given his own name and had gladly retained sufficient wits to provide Walker with my name and address, Edgar's only friend in the city.

By the time I had received the note summoning me to the Tavern, Edgar had been missing from the world for five days. The last time I had seen him was in Richmond where we had dined at Saddlers on the Friday evening five nights prior. We had both eaten a late dinner and drank lightly, I enjoyed a small beer while Edgar sipped a tea. We discussed his trip to Baltimore where I would join him later in the week. Our conversation betrayed nothing of the coming events. He was light-hearted and spoke with excitement of his recent engagement to Elmira Royster Shelton, a childhood sweetheart who he had met once more, and by chance, in Richmond. Both she and Edgar had both been widowed within the last two years and he seemed happy with the prospect of his forthcoming marriage.

Edgar's business in Baltimore was to secure some

support that had been offered from several local editing companies to publish his works. Despite being a prolific and somewhat successful writer of prose and poetry, Edgar's finances had suffered recently and the trip would hopefully prove to be a boon and a blessing for him. With dinner complete, we paid, split the checks and left sober. When he had left me to take the night boat to Baltimore, he had been in good spirits. He was dressed in his familiar, smart black wool suit, tall Regent topper, woolen scarf and black leather gloves. This evening he carried a smart silver topped Malacca cane I did not recognize. He was in a hurry, the hour was late and the midnight boat would set sail in forty-five minutes, and the docks were still a carriage ride away. At that time I had no reason to believe that I would not see Edgar in a day or so when we would meet again in Baltimore. I witnessed him step up into the carriage in the late evening mist that chilled our farewells outside Saddlers, I saw his arm wave goodbye, his carriage rounded the corner onto Hill Street and he was gone, vanished and not to be seen again for five long worry filled days.

I arrived at Gunners, winded, out of breath, cold and soaked to the skin. In my haste I had only thought to don my frock coat and it hung off my shoulders and shed rainwater around my feet. The door of the tavern was locked but I could see gas lights were still lit within. Banging on the door roused the landlord, he started at my appearance, as was typical. He was high-colored and angry at both the inconvenience and the hour. After a brief conversation and confirmation of my credentials, he allowed me entry, influenced at least partly, to be done with this unwanted business and get to his bed. The tavern was mostly empty at that hour with only a few smoky gas lights that offered illumination. The landlord introduced me curtly to Mr. Walker, the sender of the note, who had kindly waited for my arrival. He was tall, with friendly blue eyes and animated eyebrows, aged perhaps thirty, well dressed, bespectacled and sporting a neatly trimmed and fashionable Van-Dyck beard. He led me past the bar, littered with glasses and bottles, remnants from the earlier carousing, and into the shadowy parlor located in the rear of the establishment. Walker was animated and excited by the events of the evening. He recounted his tale of stumbling across my friend outside the tavern and helping him into the shelter. He talked quickly, chattering, concerned about both Edgar's disheveled condition and his disturbed mental acuity. Despite his amenable and expansive demeanor, his words and expression carried more than common concern for a fellow man laid low by some random happenstance, his voice modulated by a timbre of dread.

"Your friend has been saying the strangest things, mostly nonsense for certain, but he speaks of anguish and despair and dark things to be dreaded; I am a man usually blessed with a light heart, a man of science, but I admit his speech this night has disconcerted me."

The parlor was low ceilinged, dimly lit by a single guttering gas lamp, the creaking cheap pine floorboards spoke of a century of spilt ale and spirits, nauseous at that hour and circumstance. We found Edgar recumbent on two stained dining tables that had been roughly pulled together. The expensive Malacca cane I recognized, it was still by his side, but paradoxically his own clothes were missing. In place of his expensive suit he was now dressed in an ancient stained and tattered bombazine coat ripped at several of its seams, badly fitting black alpaca pantaloons of a similar character, a pair of coarse worn-out and muddy boots run down at the heels, and an old, tattered and ribbon-less palm leaf straw hat.

He was conscious still but muttered quietly to himself, as Walker had predicted, mostly gibberish and nonsense. His usually clear expression was furrowed and grim. Bruises ran across the right side of his face, the side closest to me and Walker, fresh contusions that still bloomed purple and black. His normally groomed and Macassar oil slicked black hair was filthy, wild and tangled. He held his hands in front of his face, repeatedly opened and closed his stained and dirty fingers and occasionally scraped and swiped at his brows as if to swat away some annoyance. His eyes were closed but as I leaned in to better hear and perhaps decipher his incoherence, his body turned slowly toward us, his left eye snapped open, bloodshot sclera with dilated ebony pupil stared wide and intently into a space behind me. A breeze from the casement window flickered the lamp and a chill descended on the room. One blackened finger uncurled a broken nail and followed the gaze that pointed a warning over my shoulder. I turned slowly to look in the direction of the staring eye and pointed finger. In the very fringe of my vision I perceived, rather than saw, a greater blackness within the darksome of the corner behind me, a vagueness that slithered and crawled across my senses. The hairs prickled on my neck, my heart raced and my eyes and ears strained to focus on the movement in their periphery. My body released adrenaline and shortened my breath to a gasp as I fully turned to face the corner; a form, dark and indistinct still lingered there, moved, writhed slowly on the edge of my awareness. As I stared, eyes wide, about to shout and raise the alarm, the shape dispersed, flickered away in the jumping shadows created by the fading lamp, revealed nothing more than an old footstool that leant against the filthy ale soiled corner of the wall behind us. The feeble swinging light from the gas lamp fooled the unreliable and limited evidence of my own senses. My tiredness and the events of the night had intruded on the practicalities of my perception for the briefest of moments.

I turned quickly back to Walker who was still chattering his animated tale without care. He seemed completely unaware of my confusion and agitated state so I shook my head to clear my unsettlement and turned my attention back to Edgar. Poor Edgar had fallen back to the table, barely conscious. He trembled as if in the beginning of a seizure so I asked Walker to quickly help hail me a cab to take us to the local hospital. Walker immediately donned his greatcoat and rushed back outside and I helped Edgar slowly and uncertainly to his feet. The landlord, whose demeanor had not improved, followed us from the parlor and watched us with a grave expression as we stepped out into the rain just as the Hansom turned the corner, a clatter of hooves on the black slick cobbles. He slammed the door behind our backs, pleased and perhaps relieved to be done with our business. From the street we could hear him shout a brusque and unnecessary, "Good night and good riddance!"

# *Chapter II*

*As of someone gently rapping, rapping at my chamber door.*
*"'Tis some visitor," I muttered, "tapping at my chamber door.*
*Only this and nothing more."*

By the time of the events at Gunners that night, I had known Edgar twenty years. We met in the year 1820, when he and his family returned from a five year trip to England. He was a year older than I, he being a stout boy of eleven and I an overly tall ten year old. We were seated at adjacent crude pine desks, ink stained and etched with the initials of a hundred bored brats, at the rear of the brightly lit classroom. The school was located above Doctor Lemonsy's shop, a hardware store on the south side of Broad Street in downtown Richmond. Our teacher was Mr. Joseph Clarke, a solid, gammon lipped and scarlet faced man, who would fluctuate from a jolly and merry mood to one of sudden anger. A passed note or a whispered secret would make his eyes appear over the brim of his spectacles, eyebrows bristling, the color rising to his cheeks. When in such a mood he was apt to quickly and surprisingly lash out with the thin birchwood cane he kept beside his uneven desk.

Edgar and I became firm friends during our schooldays and we lived close, both residing at the time in Richmond, he with his adopted parents in a long low cottage on Fifth Street, between Marshall and Clay Streets, northwest of the Capitol, and I with my father in an unpretentious residence surrounded on all sides by a row of tall linden trees, on the corner of Franklin and Second Streets.

I grew up awkwardly into a young man and attended the Hampden-Sidney College of Medicine in Virginia, earning my medical license in the year 1835. By my own admission I was not a popular child and became even less so as I grew into adulthood. I graduated medical school at the age of twenty-five and by that time I had reached the height of six feet and six inches, with long dangling limbs, thin wrists and ankles that stuck like sticks out of sleeves and cuffs. I could render the finest clothing ridiculous. I was gaunt of both body and face despite my generous diet. My eyes protruded unnervingly from my face, drew my eyelids back against my cheeks and brows, reddened my eyes, compelling me to stare menacingly even when I meant not to. It was startling to those who first met me, aggravated ten-fold by the hollowness and darkness of my cheeks.

The lank limbs, and protruding eyes were less of an inherited encumbrance, but rather the symptoms of Grave's disease. The disease had been identified by the esteemed Irish physician Robert James Graves who had recognized and grouped the symptoms I suffered. He had given them a name, if not a cure. I had started to display the symptoms when at school, prompting the children to taunt and tease me relentlessly with my apparent similarity to the then popular tale of The Legend of Sleepy Hollow and its perennially haunted and harassed hero, Ichabod Crane. The disease had continued to torture my body throughout adolescence and onward into puberty, bulging eyes, lengthening limbs and ridding me of friends and relationships.

I could not pretend that the disease and the reactions it engendered from new acquaintances had not adversely colored my personality and mood. I was known to be caustic and sarcastic in speech, and somber, if not sepulchral in personality. Without warning I could be thrown into bouts of deep depression, melancholia's taunted by raging neuralgias. I could not always tell if these bouts were symptoms of the Graves, extended social isolation or simply a flaw in my character.

My medical career had been successful despite the limitations of my appearance. I was a gifted physician and skilled surgeon and had obtained a situation at the Washington College Hospital, where I had many colleagues and acquaintances who respected my abilities, if not my humors. I had become an especially adept surgeon due to my condition being an obstacle to daily discourse with the public. The melancholia I hid from colleagues, but they largely avoided me anyway, unless they needed advice or assistance with a challenging treatment or diagnosis. In addition to my skills for saving lives, my salary had finally, and gladly, allowed me to purchase suits that were tailored by Harris's to fit my elongated frame.

It was toward the Washington College Hospital we raced, uphill on East Fayette Street in the black Hansom cab that Walker had flagged down. Stones thrown from the rough road by the horse's hooves rattled against the fender, but otherwise it was quiet inside the cab. Edgar has settled into a stupor, and leaned awkwardly against the door, a line of saliva drew a clean line across the dirt of his face. Even my excitable accomplice, Walker, who had graciously decided to see this adventure through to its conclusion had become morose, perhaps anticipating the simple anticlimax of Edgar's admission to the hospital. He stared out of the window and tapped his fingers against the door of the cab. The rain had somewhat relented and the dark clouds of night were beginning to lighten on the horizon ahead of us. The gloomy towering brick edifice of the hospital was to our right as we turned onto Broadway and then through the spiked iron gated entryway of the hospital grounds. I asked the gatekeeper to summon Doctor John J. Moran, who would be the attending physician at that hour, to meet us in the vestibule.

The vestibule was cool and vast, the domed and tiled ceiling sent the echoes of our footfalls into the heights above. Dark corridors stretched out to the east and west and a wide central stone staircase led up to the higher floors. It was here that I said farewell to Walker. He had helped me support Edgar from the cab to a heavy iron, three wheeled invalid chair that we found inside the heavy doors that guarded the entrance to the hospital.

"Thank you Mr. Walker, for helping Edgar and having the good sense to send for me. Thank you also for your assistance in getting us here safely."

"It was quite the adventure Doctor Snodgrass, I thoroughly enjoyed it but I admit I am ready for my bed," replied Walker.

"Call me Joseph," I replied, "after the events of tonight I feel we should be informal and friendly with each other if that suits you, and if it does I will call on you in a day or two, hopefully with good news about our patient?"

"It does indeed," laughed Walker, in good spirits once more, "and you shall call me William and I will look forward to your visit with pleasure."

He gave me a tired smile, we shook hands and unusually he looked me directly and candidly in the eyes. He nodded, and with shoulders rounded by fatigue walked back through the doors to take the waiting hansom back to the city.

With Edgar safely seated and strapped in the chair I pushed him squeakily across the sable tiled floor towards Doctor Moran who had entered the vestibule from the corridor that housed the examination rooms to the left. Moran was a squat man, short in height, perhaps only five feet five inches, but broad across the shoulders. His whitecoat was stretched thin across his powerful chest and his full grey beard streamed down to the monaural ebony stethoscope that hung from a silver chain around his thick neck. He had intelligent clear blue eyes behind steel rimmed circular spectacles. I liked him, as did all who worked in the hospital, he was a good man, competent, confident and cautious, not prone to excitability, a man grounded in science. In short a good physician. We spent several minutes discussing Edgar. His sudden and unexpected disappearance and the concern he had caused, how he had been found in different clothes not suiting his station, and his current tragic condition. Moran looked up toward me as he took detailed notes on the pad he kept in one of his ample pockets.

Moran admitted Edgar immediately. He summoned the night orderly, a man called Makepeace, who I knew by sight but not well. Makepeace escorted Edgar, still quiet and compliant, to a bed in a private second floor room in the tower facing the courtyard. The room was sparse by design, a bed with restraints, a small pine storage locker for the patient's clothes and personal belongings, and a tall mirror of unbreakable polished steel fastened to the wall that faced the window overlooking the court. After securing Edgar in the bed, I watched as Moran took the patients pulse and temperature. A sphygmograph was strapped around his wrist to calculate blood pressure. After all measurements were taken and duly noted on the patients chart I asked,

"Do you have any thoughts to what could have caused this terrible change in my friend."

"It is too early to make a diagnosis as you know Doctor Snodgrass," he responded cautiously. His spectacles has slipped down his nose and he paused to push them back, "but based on the story you have recanted and this obvious fugue state, I think the correct course of treatment would be too assume some form of seizure or a congestion of the brain."

"And course of treatment?"

"I think tonight we will simply monitor his condition. In the morning we can have one of the day physicians take charge and offer treatment."

I was about to argue and ask for a more immediate course of action, when our conversation was interrupted by a slow rhythmic banging from the direction of the window. Since bringing Edgar to the room he had been captivated by his reflection in the steel mirror. He seemed to have calmed himself, his own appearance, even in his sorry state, a point of focus and tranquility for his troubled mind. But now he was rocking, gently, backwards and forwards, gaze fixed on the mirror, his hands banged in time against the sides of the steel bedframe. His voice was his own but he sounded desperate and defeated.

"Ah, yes, I see you at last," he spoke sadly.

"Who do you see Edgar, I am here, your friend Joseph, is it me you see?" I asked as I took a step towards the bed and glanced back at the mirror. I looked to see what Edgar saw but it was just our reflections, peering back into the room.

Edgar began to softly chuckle to himself, still rocking.

"Edgar, who do you see?"

"I see the truth dear Joseph," spoken slowly and so forlornly, "the truth at last, after all these years of torment." His chuckling grew louder and higher in pitch.

"Tell me Edgar, I beg you, who is there, who do you see?"

Edgar moved his hands from banging the sides of the bed and started, still rocking, to slam his palms harder and harder against the sides of his head. His chuckling turned to laughter, louder and maniacal, the sound filled the echoing room. Blood began to ooze from his ears, coated the palms of his hands which continued to slam with brutal force against his poor head. Droplets of blood flew from his broken ears, his palms smeared blood across his face.

"I see you, I see you," he cackled, screaming now with laughter and glee, "at last I see you and know what you are!"

I was horrified and I admit to my shame I found myself rooted to the spot at the sight. Not so Doctor Moran who had taken action, he grabbed Edgar forcefully from behind with his left arm and deftly and expertly applied a drop mask soaked in ether over his nose and mouth with his right. Edgar struggled, but Moran's stocky strength was formidable. The rocking slowed and his muffled laughter, thankfully, began to subside. Moran continued to apply the mask until Edgar slipped backwards against him and finally down to the bed. Makepeace appeared at his shoulder, produced a syringe from his left pocket and administered a full phial of morphine into Edgar's bicep.

# *Chapter III*

*Ah, distinctly I remember it was in the bleak December.*
*And each separate dying ember wrought its ghost upon the floor.*
*Eagerly I wished the morrow; vainly I had sought to borrow…*

With Edgar thoroughly sedated and with the leather and brass buckled restraints of his bed now tightened around his wrists and ankles, I followed Moran down the echoing corridor towards the office shared by the attending Doctors. The room was small and cramped, a leather topped oak desk and faded wingback leather chesterfield, mounted on castors, dominated the space. An old and scratched wooden spindled chair was provided for visitors. A small gas hob and pot stood cold on the shelf by the small window that overlooked the hospital entrance. Light streamed into the room and I guessed the time must have been close to eight in the morning. Books and manuscripts crowded the shelves behind the desk, A Treatise on Human Anatomy, Maclise's Surgical Anatomy and Bennet's Clinical Lectures on Principals of Medicine. Old friends, wrinkled with greasy well-thumbed and turned down pages. I had entered first and instinctively sat in the comfy chesterfield. Moran immediately bristled.

"My chair, thank you Snodgrass."

"It has been a long night Moran, the chair is fine," I motioned him towards the spindle chair.

"I am the attending physician at this hour and the night has been a long one for all of us. If you cannot for once be respectful Snodgrass, you may leave this office forthwith and consider our business concluded."

I sat for a moment, angry and obstinate but I knew deep down that protocol lay on his side. Finally I stood and we shuffled awkwardly around the desk to exchange places. I took my place in the uncomfortable wooden chair with a grunt.

Moran dumped his heavy body into the Chesterfield

making it roll back several inches away from the desk, and I perched awkwardly on the chair, seated lower but still towering over the good Doctor.

Moran skirted the chair once more back toward the desk and leant on its stained and scratched leather surface. He steepled his fingers to support his head and let out a sigh of fatigue and concern. I let out a sigh of my own and tried to calm myself from the residue of fear and turmoil, remnants of the violent furor in Edgar's room. I swallowed my pride and suppressed my characteristic tendency toward another caustic response.

"I apologize Doctor, the office is your own and you did well, better than I. I truly appreciate your speedy intervention, may we continue to talk?"

"Very well, if we can both remain professional," he said, "let us begin by discussing the patient's history. You have known Edgar for how long?"

"For twenty years, we went to school together for a number of years and have been friend's and correspondents ever since."

"Then let's start there if you would Doctor Snodgrass. Tell me this poor man's story and perhaps we can between us, divine some clues as to what has brought him to this dark divide?"

Moran turned to the pot and started to brew a cup of sustenance. The night had truly been long for both of us and the story I was to share would take us through the remainder of the morning. I shifted uncomfortably in the small chair and began to disclose to Moran what I knew of Edgars life.

"The story that I had heard of the family prior to my meeting Edgar at school, was that both his father and mother were entertainers. Elizabeth Arnold was an actress who achieved sporadic success on the stages of Boston and Charleston. She had married David Poe, also an actor, less successful and with a career stifling habit of threatening with violence any critic who spared a harsh word for his abilities." I paused to reflect for a moment, "the same fault in his character that Edgar occasionally displays with literary critics, now I think about it."

"Was the marriage a good one?"

"It was not, it was in fact a tragic one. David deserted Elizabeth and their three young children, and shortly afterwards Elizabeth died destitute, finally succumbing to the consumption that had plagued that last year of her young life. In a cruel twist of fate, David died of the same dread disease only a year later."

"What of the children, what happened to them?"

"There were three children as I say, Henry, the eldest, Edgar and his younger sister Rosalie. They were each broken up between different households. Young Edgar, only two at the time added the surname of his adoptive family and became Edgar Allan Poe. The Allan's were comfortably wealthy. At that time I believe they lived above the trading store they owned in Richmond. John Allan was originally Scottish and it was to Livingston the family, including Edgar, returned to sometime during the summer of 1815. Edgar would have been six at the time. He told me later that he spent time in schools in Livingston as well as London. In 1820 the family returned to the United Colonies and Richmond. It was in that year, in the little school above Doctor Lemonsy's store that I first met him. I remember him as being athletic, a strong swimmer and competitive boxer, a decent student, well advanced in Latin and a lover of the classics. I recall him reading Horace and Cicero's Orations in Latin and Homer in Greek. From what I could tell, his home life was agreeable although his mother had shown signs of sickness and there were some minor frictions between himself and his adopted father."

I paused to sip on the tea that Moran had kindly brewed. I let the steam rise to my face, savoring the freshness and reviving aromas. Moran was unusual in his penchant for tea, most of the medical staff relied on coffee to get through the day, but still, it tasted good at that hour.

"So some early tragedy, the loss of a mother and father at such a young age, yet his teenage life seemed to provide the stability he would need?" Moran asked, sipping his tea.

"Unfortunately things were about to change for the worst I am afraid. He was eighteen and at college, the University of Virginia, when there was a scandal concerning gambling and a debt unpaid. Edgar never did confide in me the truth of the matter, but it split Edgar from his adopted father for many years. He left college, or perhaps was told to leave. I only know that he joined the military for a while, but he always had an independent streak and that only lasted a year or so. It was around that time that Edgar began to write, poetry at first and then some prose."

"Was he successful, did his work get published?"

"He had some poetry published, it was titled Tamerlane I believe but resulted in no success."

"So, he left the military, what then?"

"When he was twenty-one he lost his eldest brother Henry. It was at the time of the cholera outbreak, if you remember that terrible year, 1831 I seem to recall, but there was also a rumor of alcohol."

"How did Edgar take the loss?"

"Badly I think, but it did result in Edgar writing a conciliatory letter to his father and they were re-united soon after. He worked for various newspapers and continued to write his poetry, still with little success. He married in 1836, more scandal I am afraid. Her name was Virginia Clemm, she was his first cousin and only thirteen at the time."

"Good heavens, thirteen! Wait, you say 'was,' is she dead then?"

"Sadly so, at the age of eighteen she began to bleed from the mouth while playing the piano, five years later she was no more."

"The romantic disease, just like his mother and father."

"As you say Doctor, consumption, the slow killer of our age. It devasted poor Edgar and I am sorry to say he turned to the evils of drink for many months. He had at this point achieved some notoriety as a writer. His wife's long illness perhaps, had provided some dark inspiration, as his long poem 'The Raven' had been published and received some acclaim. Have you read the poem Doctor Moran?"

"I have not. My time is consumed by medical journals I'm afraid Doctor Snodgrass, I have no time for literary trifles."

"You should read it Doctor, it is a dark tale, perhaps an insight into a mind already troubled. A clue perchance to what we seek, a window into his sorry condition. I have a copy at my home, I will bring it to you tomorrow."

"Very well Doctor Snodgrass. And what then with our patient, how does the tale end?"

"Last year he met again his childhood sweetheart, a lady named Elmira Shelton. She had lost her husband a year or so earlier and following a brief courtship they became engaged. To my knowledge they were both happy and were anticipating their imminent betrothal. That brings us almost to the current date and situation. I dined with Edgar five, well, let me consider, I guess now it would be six nights ago in Richmond. I saw him climb into the Hansom cab that would take him to the docks from where he was to catch the midnight boat here to Baltimore. He then went missing for five nights and was rescued by a young gentleman called William Walker who sent for me. Now here we are."

The room was silent for some time while we both considered the facts, the life of a man laid bare in so few words. Moran was about to rise to brew some fresh tea when there came a disturbance at the door.

"What is it Makepeace?" asked Moran.

"Sorry to interrupt sir, but I thought you should see this."

With that the man stepped into the room. I wrinkled my nose, his body odor was sour, perhaps due to a long shift, but I was unimpressed. His clothing too was shabby, stained and wrinkled. For the first time I took time to ascertain the character of the man. He was swarthy, short in the body but with long arms. He had a long hooked nose topped by small grey eyes, his mouth a lipless downturned slit in his face. His hirsute hand, with cracked and dirty nails held the handsome silver topped Malacca cane.

"What of it Makepeace?" I asked curtly, angered by the audacity of the man and the rudeness of his appearance, "we know all about the cane."

With that Makepeace shifted the shaft of the cane to his left hand and with his right swept a sword from the concealed hilt, a lethal looking three feet of white steel.

"A swordstick," gasped Moran.

"Another mystery," I said.

"Are those marks on the blade?" asked Moran as he leant across the desk.

"They look like symbols, runes and such nonsense," I answered, "signs of the occult perhaps."

"A mystery most certainly," replied Makepeace, speaking in awe, almost under his breath, "but perhaps one that can be solved. There is also an inscription on the blade."

I grabbed the handle of the sword to wrest it from Makepeace's grip. I turned the blade carefully over until I found the inscription. It was faintly engraved, set amidst myriad sigils, in a flowing and elaborate copperplate script:

*Doctor John F. Carter*

"John Carter, I know of that man" shouted Moran, more animated than I had seen him in many years, "he is a charlatan, a shyster, a quack and mountebank. A dabbler in the paranormal."

"How do you know him, have you had business with him?"

"I have, he swindled my sister out of $300 only two years since. A fake séance and a promise of a connection to her late husband, and he is no Doctor," Moran scoffed.

"Then you know where he resides?"

"I do! Well his offices anyway. He carries out what he calls business at Seventh and Broad Streets, in Richmond."

# *Chapter IV*

*From my books surcease of sorrow—sorrow for the lost Lenore—*
*For the rare and radiant maiden whom the angels name Lenore—*
*Nameless here for evermore.*

I bade Moran farewell. It was noon, the poor Doctor was five hours past the end of his shift and for the time being he had done all that he could do. I wanted to check on Edgar's condition before I left, so made my way, swordstick in hand, back down the now busy corridor toward his room on the second floor. I dodged orderlies and nurses who carried linen bags and pushed wheeled gurneys down the black and white tiled hallway. I received curt nods of acknowledgement from some of the staff and an occasional muttered 'good afternoon,' to which I sent my customary bad natured grunt in reply.

Edgar was as I had left him, unconscious and secured by the straps around his wrists and ankles. I checked that the straps were not too tight and took a moment to check his condition. To the nursing staff's credit he had been well attended too. His bruises and wounds had been neatly dressed and he had been washed, the grime from his battered face and hands replaced by the sweet antiseptic tang of carbolic. Pure white bandages wound around his head, secured gauze dressings over his newly damaged ears. His filthy clothes had been removed and stored with his few belongings. He had been changed into green and white striped flannel pajamas. I listened to his breathing for a moment, still ragged and thready, he was murmuring quietly under his breath. I leaned in close, my ear almost up against his mouth. I believed I could just make out a word, perhaps a name?

"Rey…nold," he whispered, "Reynold…"

"Edgar, can you hear me, who is Reynold?"

His breath rattled and the words faded to silence, I listened until all I could hear was the blood pounding in my own ears but there was only silence. A sudden crash behind me made me leap upright and suppress an exclamation of fright. Makepeace had entered behind me, had banged a trolley, filled with clanging bedpans and metal jugs of water, against the door to the room. My nerves were on a precipitous edge and I was embarrassed at my own discomfiture.

"Jumping Piminy you oaf!"

"I beg your pardon Doctor, my apologies, I didn't intend to give you fright."

I was about to storm angrily and rudely past him but a moment of guilt and concern for Edgar gave me pause, "You surprised me, that is all," I took a breath to calm my anger, "I wanted to thank you Makepeace, for taking good care of this unfortunate soul."

"It is my duty Doctor Snodgrass. One thing Doctor if I might?"

"Yes, of course, what is it?"

"I took the liberty of covering the mirror. It seemed to disturb your friend. Whenever he woke he would try and sit up against his restraints and stare into it. I hope that I didn't do wrong?"

I looked for the first time back at the where the polished steel mirror hung from the wall opposite the window. A rough hessian green bedspread had been thrown across it, tucked carelessly behind at the corners to temporarily secure it.

"It was all I could find in my haste to calm your friend."

"You did well Makepeace, I thank you. This poor soul has been my friend for many years and I may be away for a number of days; it would ease my mind if I knew that you were to continue in his care?"

"You have my word Doctor."

I whispered a goodbye to Edgar and patted his shoulder although there was no sign that he knew I was there. With that, I nodded my farewell to Makepeace, walked down the long stone steps, through the vestibule and stepped back into the hospital grounds. The cool of a Baltimore afternoon in fall greeted me. I inhaled deeply, my exhale condensed into a mist in the chill of the day. In and out, slowly repeated, released the stress and anxiety of the previous night. People were going about their business, walking up Broadway toward the town, shopping, talking. Just a normal afternoon, the sun low and watery in the clear blue sky, the streets still glistening from the previous evenings storm. A dark bay gelding was pulling a Hansom cab up the hill toward me, breath snorted steam with the effort. It approached and I hailed the driver. The coach tilted on the creaking sprung iron leaf suspension as I stepped up, and bent my awkward frame into the cab, and I rode it, exhausted back to my apartment on High Street.

I badly needed sleep. I intended to take the night boat to Richmond that very evening to meet with this Doctor Carter, but wanted to speak with William Walker before I left. I sent a runner to Walker's address asking him if he would be so good as to meet me at Martick's, my favorite restaurant on West Mulberry Street, close to the Inner Harbor, at seven o'clock for dinner. With the note dispatched, I wound my way up the creaking spiral stairway and into my little bedroom. The room was dark, curtains still drawn against the night of the previous evening, my bedclothes strewn on the floor, a remnant of being rudely woken by the boy with the summoning note. I set Edgar's cane carefully down by my nightstand and sat on my low bed, let out a groan as I bent double to remove my calf skin stovepipe boots and with eyes already closing, lent my long and aching body back against the creaking bedframe and chased madness and violence along black and white tiled corridors down toward sleep.

I woke from a fitful slumber before five thirty in the evening with a neuralgia and sore scratchy eyes. The Grave's disease had caused my eyes to dry, but in the water closet by my bed I poured some cold water from the blue and white patterned jug into the matching bowl and splashed my face to refresh them and chase the last of the sleep from my face. I packed lightly, a travel trunk would be unnecessary on this short trip, my trusty carpet bag, dark green with brass locking plate would be more than sufficient for the few clothes and wash items that would be needed. With my worsted suit, greatcoat and black topper donned, I grabbed my carpet bag and Edgar's mysterious cane and left the house.

I arrived at Martick's at precisely seven o'clock to find William smiling at my arrival, already seated at my favorite table. The table was in the back of the crowded restaurant, away from the windows at the front, that would otherwise draw looks of amusement and horror in equal measure in my direction from passersby. We ordered a Vitis Labrusca wine, seasoned with fresh herbs and spices and fermented locally at the Brotherhood winery on the outskirts of the city. I took some moments to bring William up to speed with the events since he had left the hospital. He was horrified when I recounted Edgar's crazed violence toward himself, but was hugely intrigued by the tale of the cane and its hidden blade. I showed it to him under the table, extracted three inches of white steel from the sheath, enough to display the mysterious etchings and inscription. William gasped and stared in awe at the blade and its hidden meanings.

I told him of my plan, to visit this 'Doctor' Carter in Richmond the following morning. "I take the night boat back to Richmond tonight, in a little over two hours-time. In all the time I have known him, Edgar never once mentioned a Doctor Carter to me, and I intend to understand if there is a link between the swordstick and Edgar's disappearance. I think Carter may have the answers."

To my eternal surprise he clasped my right hand in both of his.

"If you would allow it Joseph, I will accompany you on

this endeavor. It could prove perilous for one person alone, and I confess, I am intrigued and in need of adventure."

I was taken aback, but at the same time, no small part of me was thankful for the offer of assistance. My usual response would be to flatly refuse, but his lightness of spirit and eagerness to help overcame my natural hesitancy. If I was honest with myself, although the venture carried a notion of intrigue, I was deeply trepidatious of the task ahead, filled with apprehension. Whatever dark forces had preyed on Edgar and brought him to that sorry state were potent and entirely puissant. I didn't believe for a moment they were paranormal in origin, more likely a symptom of narcotics or general malaise, nonetheless my penchant for melancholy left me in a reflective and dark brooding mood.

"I don't know you well at all William, we met only last night," I started.

"Wait, listen to me Joseph…"

"You interrupt me too soon William, if you will let me continue?"

William tilted his head, an unspoken apology and consent to speak.

"Although I don't know you well, I believe you to be a good and honest man and I would accept your offer of assistance gladly. You would be a most welcome companion."

We both smiled and clinked our wine glasses and sipped the wine.

"You will need some change of clothing I think, we may be gone more than a day or two. I know not what we will find in Richmond."

He stood briskly, "I will return home to pack immediately and I will meet you at the docks."

"The Paddle Steamer leaves from Pier 4 on East Pratt Street at Ten sharp."

William picked up his top hat and gloves and brusquely

left the restaurant. The dock was but a short walk from Martick's so I ordered my usual bowl of lamb broth and crust and took a moment to reflect on the events since I had been summoned to Gunners, and to plan the imminent meeting with Carter. The restaurant was warm, a soft flickering glow from the candles in the rear created a charming ambience. My food arrived and it was, as always, piping hot and peppery, the lamb tender and greasy and the bread crusty and slavered in salty yellow butter. The clatter of the cutlery and the chatter of the diners calmed my mind, the wine dulled my thoughts. It was nine thirty when I left, I wound my way carefully through the crowded tables, ignored the stares and whispered comments, and stepped back onto the now darkened street of West Mulberry. I paused for a moment to look back at the warm welcoming glow through the windows. I wished at that moment that if I could have had a notion of the events that lay ahead of me, I swear, I would have returned to my little table in the back and never left.

# Chapter V

*And the silken, sad, uncertain rustling of each purple curtain*
*Thrilled me—filled me with fantastic terrors never felt before;*
*So that now, to still the beating of my heart, I stood repeating…*

The paddle steamer *Francis* was readying to depart from Pier 4. Black smoke reached high into the cold night sky from the two towering black smokestacks close to her prow. She lay low in the water, her twin decks were wrapped by ornate iron railings forged to resemble white picket fencing. A row of portholes lay close to the waterline, marked out the locations of the staterooms. The Pier was alive with throngs of passengers, stevedores and stewards, piles of luggage and last minute provisions, kegs and barrels, boxes and crates, all ready to be loaded for the twelve hour voyage to Richmond. I searched through the crowds for William Walker, my height lending me advantage, and spied him by the gang plank. He in turn was looking for me, scanning the teeming crowds. I pushed my way through the press of bodies, mindful of pickpockets who would certainly be working in this mix on such a night, and met him with a shake of hands and an honest smile.

We walked up the creaking and slippery wooden gang plank located below the towering smoke-stacks. The ship was already crowded, we had to jostle our way to the stern to negotiate with the ticketing steward. We were in luck and took possession of two handsome staterooms. The stairs down into the hull were steep, they led to two long corridors that ran the length of the ship, one to port and one to starboard. The staterooms were well lit, each with a small gas light, the rooms spacious, white paneled with gilded molding. I stored my carpet bag beside the small bed and secreted the cane beneath the mattress. No sooner had I stored my meagre belongings than a bell rang out, the ships horn blew a loud mournful howl, long and low into the night, the boilers shook the vessel and rattled the fixtures, and I could feel the water moving below me. I knocked on Williams's door and together we climbed up and out onto the deck of the Francis in time to see the last heavy hawser being thrown ashore. The enormous paddles on each side of the ship slowly started to churn the water below them, the harnessed force of steam struggling to overcome the mass and inertia of the river below. The horn blew again, ear splitting at that remove and we were underway, the bow swung away from the pier, severed our tie to land. Water surged under the paddles and the Francis began the careful navigation into the Inner harbor of the oily black Patapsco River.

With a shiver against the chill of the night we stepped back inside and took a table by a window in the dining saloon, elegant with imported Belgian carpets, sumptuous velvet chairs with marble-topped tables. I took stock of my new young friend in the kinder surroundings of the ship's saloon. He was fresh faced, his spectacles thin wire, framed around his clear blue gaze. Blond hair swept forward, almost covering his right eye, his beard was as neatly trimmed as I remember. I realized, perhaps much too late given the nature of our circumstance, that I knew almost nothing of his history and background. We ordered a bottle of Jules Robin cognac, and while I poured a measure each into the crystal shot classes I asked him to tell me his story.

"There is not much of a tale to tell Joseph and it is not a particularly happy one, but you are welcome to have it." William sat back, took a sip of brandy and licked his lips,

"I was born in this city twenty-nine years ago, the son of a Baltimore policeman. My mother I never knew, she sadly died in childbirth. My grandmother raised me really, my father busy with his work." He paused to pick at the cotton wool of his memories, "in truth he was always distant with me, he was a strong, tough man and struggled to show emotion. I suspect I carried the blame of his broken heart and years of loneliness, a constant noisy and needy reminder of his loss."

The river rolled darkly by outside the window, the lights of the inner harbor faded slowly as the steamer picked its careful way between the ships anchored in the bay.

"My grandmother, my mother's mother, saw a resemblance in me to her. It has been said I have her face. While it softened her heart toward me, it hardened his, he could barely stand to look at me or be in my presence. As well as a daily reminder of his loss I was also a disappointment to him. I was a less than average student at an above average school, my grades were poor and there was some trouble, fist fights with some of the other boys who teased me for only having a grandmother. By the time I turned thirteen we had drawn an unspoken line between us." He paused to drain his glass. I leant across and topped off both of our glasses, the brandy shone the color of burnt cinnamon in the low lights of the saloon, the crystal sent bright splashes of light across the table. The dining room was filling up and we were cocooned by the noise, the excited hubbub of the other travelers and the dim lights and shifting shadows from the candles on the tables. He took another sip and continued.

"There was always tension between us. My father wanted me to follow him into the police force, but I decided instead upon a military career. I still couldn't tell you if that was what I truly wanted, or if I just wanted to hurt him, forever intent to disappoint. The day I was to leave my childhood home and set off alone for the Academy was also the day I turned seventeen. He came down the stairs in his uniform to find me packing my few belongings. He left for work, walked silently past me. Despite the gulf we had placed deliberately and carefully between us, through long years, his leaving in that manner broke my heart. I didn't at the time consider that my leaving broke his, but I took his cue and we never spoke again.

"I graduated from West Point Academy three years later and became a cavalry officer in the regular army. For the first four years of my service I was stationed in Fort Arnold itself, a dull and endlessly repetitive routine of drills and night watches." He paused to collect his thoughts once more, glanced at the lights of the city skyline behind the silhouette of Fort McHenry that receded into the darkness of the night. His brow furrowed, there was a long drawn out silence, and I let him consider his introspection.

"Then I was called to war. The campaign to force the Seminole tribes out of Florida and into the Indian Reservations that lay between the Appalachians and the Mississippi, was going badly. The Seminole's had adopted guerrilla tactics, picking off individual soldiers then vanishing into the wilderness. The Army was losing too many good soldiers. General Jesup was appointed to take command of the campaign and he immediately adopted a much more aggressive stance, more soldiers were needed and I was to be one of that number."

His usually frank and open expression darkened, the ships lights on the water reflected back from his cobalt blue eyes. "Jesup tired quickly of chasing lone Seminole warriors through the mangrove and steamy Floridian swamps."

"What tactics did he adopt William?"

"It is my young life's regret to have to tell you of my part in that Joseph, but I shall…" He looked forlornly down at the glass between his hands, the familiar smile had slipped away, his hair hung down to cover his face, but after a moment he raised his chin to look me once more squarely in the eye. "Murder, Joseph, a carnage, the butchering of men, women and infants. Jesup ordered attacks on their homes, the villages and farms of the Seminole. We were to kill without discrimination, our mission was eradication using muskets and swords against a tribe armed with only simple knives and a few wooden arrows…a massacre."

"You were following orders William."

"Yes, and I have told myself that again and again, night after night Joseph, but it only salves the conscience for so long. Now I am haunted, nightly, by the face of those women and children who turned, running in panic and fear, to look me in the eye as I rode to cut them down." His eyes were moist and he wiped a sleeve across his face and took a deep gulp of the brandy. "I am sorry Joseph, the memory, the terror is still so fresh."

There was a long silence between us, I didn't know how to offer consolation. I had had so little practice in my lonely existence, that the pain of another was as removed as love from these tortured bones and empty soul of mine. I had been absent from the family of the common man for too long, I had no compassion to share. With nothing to offer in terms of sympathy or comfort all I could do to offer succor was to help him end his tale.

"What finished your service?"

"Ha, now that at last is a story worth telling!" He smiled sadly but I was pleased, nonetheless, to see it return. He raised his left hand to his brow and swept the hair back from his right eye. A deep ugly, furrowed scar creased from the start of his hairline back across his skull. "A musket ball, shot by our own troops, careless in their aim. Luckily it merely creased me but still it nearly split my skull. Put me in a coma for a week and earned me my honorable discharge certificate and a handsome Army Captain's pension."

I smiled, "now that I can raise a toast to," we clinked our glasses, "to a Captain's pension!"

We both chuckled for a moment. It was a sad story but I felt that a gap had closed, strangers and companions become true friends.

"And now, what is it you do with your life and your pension?"

"I live a quietly boring and dangerously tedious life,

alone in Baltimore. When I returned home I found that my father had died during my absence, we never did get a chance to reconcile. He must have loved me in the end, the house was full of newspaper clippings of my graduation and small honors, he had followed my career most closely. I have nobody else who relies on my survival." He looked at me directly, "I do believe Joseph that finding Edgar that night, and you agreeing to my assistance today, may have saved my sanity if not my life."

# *Chapter VI*

*"'Tis some visitor entreating entrance at my chamber door—*
*Some late visitor entreating entrance at my chamber door;—*
*This it is and nothing more."*

I woke with a scream in my throat, gasping for breath, the sheets sweat soaked, the night terrors snapping at my heels, an anvil on my chest. The scene remained livid in front of me, two hooded jaundiced eyes, the hircine pupils a dark gash, reflected my own face, horror stricken, mouth a rictus howl of terror. There had been murky bottle green water, long streaming pondweed reaching out, snaring, wrapping my hands, arms and legs. The water pulled me deeper into the darkness and the weeds, slimy and glutinous slipped around my neck and tightened to a noose. Unable to move, paralyzed, I looked up and saw above me a water distorted moon, crescent bright, rising from behind an ancient ruin, a castle or a church. Beneath me was only darkness and death and still I descended to my fate. The blackness enveloped me and my vision narrowed to a pinprick. And then the eyes. They appeared faint, far below me, glowed with a sickly yellow light in the gloom, but quickly, oh so quickly they ascended, headed, rushed upward toward me, to capture me, to devour me. I struggled against the hold of the weeds, burning oxygen, panic consumed me, the blood screamed in my veins, the beast was upon me, I could see my face reflected in the jaundiced pupils, screaming…

My breathing was ragged, my pulse raced, totally disoriented. The sweat soaked sheets fooled my senses, convinced me for a moment that I was still in the grip of the water, drowning in the murk and being pursued by the beast. I blinked and rubbed my sore eyes, it was still night-time, perhaps an hour or two toward morning. The dark stateroom surrounded me and the regular vibration and hum of the boilers rooted me back to the present and anchored me slowly but gladly back to reality. In my bunk, safe from harm, just a nightmare. A nightmare like nothing I had experienced, true, but still just a nightmare. The night terror was hard to shake, it retained its grip on my nerves. I released the breath I had been holding and concentrated instead on the steady thrum of the engines, the hushed footsteps of a night porter busy about his work in the corridor outside, the mundane nighttime noises of the steamer, I slowly regained control of my respiration and pulse.

The evenings brandy had been a mistake, my head was sore and my mouth a scorched, arid desert. My throat a cactus, parched, but I lacked sufficient spittle to swallow. The gentle motion of the ship as it cut its way along the Chesapeake threatened to bring bile to my mouth and my gorge to rise. Still sweating and trembling I threw my legs out of the bed. They were cramped and aching, I had slept awkwardly, the cabin bed a good six inches too short for my comfort. There would be no more sleep for me that night and dawn was on its way, so I decided to leave the cabin and go in search of coffee to quell my nausea and revive my spirits.

The dining saloon was lit, the staff were busy setting up tables with clinking glasses and rattling cutlery, readying the room for breakfast. I found the kitchen closed, but after some harsh words they petulantly acquiesced, grumpily recognized that the easiest way to rid me from their presence was to furnish me with my brew. With hands cupped and warming, and my greatcoat pulled up around my ears, faint curses and impertinent comments regarding my appearance behind me, I stood shivering on the deck. The steamer cut a shimmering line across the broad and black Chesapeake Bay, while I stood cold and stooped, waiting for the light to appear on the port side of the ship

The earth below me slowly turned, quietly cast the dawn into the sky, illuminated the landscape and scattered shadows across the water. The long sandy beaches of Cape Charles sprang into sight as the sun finally freed itself of the horizon, set flame to the sky, a vivid crimson and orange canvas for the long streaming dove white cirrocumulus. The steamer began a slow turn to starboard, headed toward the inlet of the James River. The sun dappled water streamed along the hull of the ship, and the gulls called and mewed to each other as they swooped into the troubled wake behind the ships churning paddles. The slight warmth from the first touch of the sun and the sounds of the river eased my mind and stilled the memory of the night's terror. The old settlement of Jamestown was to starboard, and as we drew level, the steamer cut power in preparation for the difficult navigation of the narrow and twisting river passage. The boat slowed immediately and settled deeper into the river as we passed under the arching wooden York bridge that marked the approach to our destination.

I found William at breakfast in the dining saloon. He was seated at the same table we had occupied the previous evening. Unlike myself, he looked fresh and ready for action, his younger years had allowed him to recover from the brandy without consequence. I took a seat across from him and we said our good mornings. He was eating a huge and splendid breakfast, soft poached eggs, golden yolks that spilled across asparagus tips piled high on hot buttered toast, followed by English muffins and salted crackers accompanied by a tangy and crumbly Roquefort to finish. Fresh squeezed orange juice and hot black, smoke bitter coffee were standing by in tall pots. I ordered a plain omelet, and when it arrived, churlishly half thrown on the table by one of the waiting staff I had harangued earlier in the morning, I picked at it, swallowed carefully and tested each bite to see if it would heal or harm my constitution. Not a word was spoken until knives and forks were back on plates and the coffee pot emptied. After we both settled back in our chairs, William with a contented sigh and I with a quiet groan and suppressed belch, I apprised William of my nightmare.

William looked worried at the tale, his smile replaced by a frown, he leant toward me pushed his spectacles back up to the bridge of his nose, "surely just a nightmare, nothing to concern us and our mission?"

"It felt so real William, vivid in texture and detail, almost a premonition or…memory. I don't know what to make of it."

"Well, we will arrive in Richmond within the hour Joseph. What do we know of this Doctor Carter?"

"Almost nothing. The best that Moran could offer was that he is an occultist, a necromancer of some sort, but Moran also believed him to be a charlatan."

"Do we have a plan, if this dream of your is indeed a premonition, and this Carter fellow dabbles in demonology, I feel we may be stepping, nay, sprinting out of our depth?"

I smiled wryly "I would hesitate to call anything we are doing a plan William." I took a moment to consider our courses of action. The breakfast had done its job, I was starting to feel myself again, the terrors of the night dispelled somewhat, confidence and a readiness for action took their place.

"There are two mysteries I am hoping to resolve. If the cane is indeed the property of this Doctor Carter, as the inscription would lead us to believe, how did it come into the hands of Edgar."

And the second?"

"What is Edgar's relationship with Carter? I have known Edgar a long time and I have never heard his name or seen the cane before. If he did indeed get the swordstick from Carter, that meeting may have been the same night he disappeared, the night we dined together in Richmond."

"Well, there are two of us, and together I have to believe we will make a most excellent team."

I gave a laugh in response, "let us hope so, this may be a fool's errand, but there is a chance that it may have a bearing on the events that led to Edgar's disappearance and current illness. I think we must take the direct approach and simply confront this Carter with the facts, and judge him on his responses."

We left the saloon, promised to meet once more in the booth once the ship was docked. I returned to my stateroom and retrieved the cane from under the mattress. My hands tremored a little as I slowly unsheathed a quarter of the blade and examined it in the watery light that danced off the river that illuminated the room. The white steel was remarkable, flawless in its creation, intricately etched with arcane symbols impossible to decipher, their purpose unfathomable to me. I ran my finger across the flat of the blade, traced the whorls and patterns of the elaborate and obscure designs. I could only hope that perhaps our meeting with Doctor Carter would remove the shroud from the insoluble and provide some answers to the questions pertaining to Edgar's condition, and why he had come to have such a handsome and valuable thing in his possession.

The ships bell rang out a call for action, answered by the ships horn blaring once more its loud mournful note across the harbor. I could feel the ships direction change below me, tight turns as the ship approached harbor. Out of my little window I could see the tops of tall sails that danced with rigging, as seabirds twisted in the air. The steam engines powered down, the rush of the water over the paddles receded, silence descended. We had arrived in the city of Richmond.

# *Chapter VII*

*Presently my soul grew stronger; hesitating then no longer,*
*"Sir," said I, "or Madam, truly your forgiveness I implore;*
*But the fact is I was napping, and so gently you came rapping…*

The steamer pulled slowly into its berth alongside the tall sailing ships, some preparing to set sail, other with sails furled. Stevedores and merchants crowded the docks, hauled heavy bales of cotton and tobacco from the red brick five story warehouses that ran the length of the harbor. Mayo's bridge sat low in the water, the wide green James river slipped slowly by before it was rendered to a spray and whitewater foam over the rocky shoals west of Mayo Island. The low green hill of Richmond rose from the dock road toward the center of the city, crowned by the white columns and porticos of the Capitol Building on the horizon. Lines, heavy salt crusted coils were thrown from the dock and tightly tethered, secured the ship back to the land.

I made my way through the ship's corridors toward the saloon, crowded now with passengers rushing to disembark, encumbered by baggage and luggage. As usual William was waiting with a smile in the booth I now considered to be our own. Our plan was to walk directly to Carter's offices on the corner of Seventh and Broad Streets. We disembarked, pushed along the gangplank by the surging throng. The morning was pleasant, the sun provided some fall warmth, but a cold breeze had followed us down the James River from the Chesapeake and the Atlantic beyond and I tightened my greatcoat and pitched my black topper against the chill. The walk took us uphill, up streets lined with elms, fall leaves the color of copper and gold. We passed the gloomy brown Masonic Hall on nineteenth street and then turned left onto Franklin and stood for a moment to look in admiration at the green lawn that led to the shining white edifice of the Capitol

Building, its six Corinthian columns and marble portico blinded our eyes in the low sun. Behind us we could look back down onto the green snake of the James River sprinkled with white canvas sails bringing commerce to the city. As we walked on, the tension became palpable between us, the moment to confront this Carter and wrest the facts from him imminent. Turning North onto seventh street brought into view the vast tall Marshall theater. The offices of Doctor Carter were across the road in front of us, it was time to confront this necromancer and ascertain his character.

The office was inauspicious, a faded black door with scratched and tarnished brass furniture. The single window-pane faced south back toward the river, but the glass had been blackened. We peered in but the interior was invisible from the street. A plaque, black with white recessed lettering was screwed to the wall by the door and stated simply:

*Doctor Carter*
*Theosophist,*
*Occultist,*
*Geomancer,*
*Astrologer*

I glanced a question across at William who gave me a shrug and a resigned grin in answer, we had come this far and despite our fears there was only one course of action, so I twisted the brass doorknob, pushed the door open and stepped inside. No doorbell clanged to tell of our presence. Papers and letters littered the floor by the door. The interior was as dark as the window suggested, the sunlight of the day banned from that space. There was an aged wooden round table to our left surrounded by four spindle back chairs. The walls bare, the wallpaper damp and peeling in places. The floor was dusty and ancient, rotting, creaking pine floorboards. There was a counter at the back of the small space, behind which was a card stuck crudely to the wall with yellow peeling tape at each corner. The card was badly handwritten, a scrawling, sloppy penmanship that detailed the charges for various services, fortune telling, tarot, banishing's, crystal gazing, necromancy. A most inauspicious beginning, not the mysterious and potentially dangerous lair we had been in dread of.

There was a door to the rear, behind the counter. William looked in my direction and I nodded consent. He walked silently around the desk, careful to not step on the loosest boards. This time William turned the door handle and pushed but the room was locked.

"Look for a key." I said.

The counter had several draws and shelves, but other than one that stored some long pins and rubber bands, they were dust filled and empty. William looked around the space, moved the table and chairs and walked slowly around the walls. Nothing was revealed until he pulled the card from where it had been taped to the wall behind the counter. He looked closely at the list of services offered and seeing no clues, flipped the card over and immediately shouted me over.

On the back of the card in a flowing and elegant penmanship was written '*cellula secreto*.' He looked at me perplexed and handed me the card.

"It is written in Latin. It spells 'A Secret Compartment.' But where I wonder…"

William walked back to the counter and pulled the drawer that held the pins and rubber bands. He turned it over emptied the contents onto the counter and examined the wooden bottom of the drawer.

"It feels too heavy," he said, weighing it in his hand. He pushed a fingernail into the space where the base met the drawer front and with the slightest of leverage the base slipped backwards to reveal a cramped space beneath, just large enough to secrete the iron key that fell to the floor at his feet.

William smiled a wicked grin and quickly bent to retrieve the key and slid it into the lock and turned. The door screeched open on rusted hinges, making us both wince. If there had been a malign presence it would have been very much aware of our being there. William decided on bravado and stepped boldly through and I followed close behind, swordstick in hand.

The door opened onto a long room lit by barred windows that ran along the length of the far wall. Sunbeams fell through the bars to fall upon dust motes that floated through the space. It seemed that the front office was a stage, a trick to deceive the occasional passerby. This room was puzzling and arcane, filled with a vast collection of objects, heavy tapestries lined the walls, suits of ancient polished armor stood vigil beside them gleaming in the sunshine. Crowns and girdles hung from racks. A long glass case housed a collection of swords, some rusted and notched, others that shone like they had been newly forged. Row upon row of ancient jugs, urns and cauldrons lay about the space. Books without number lined bookcases that stretched almost to the ceiling. I walked across and ran my finger along several of the wrinkled leather spines as I whispered their names 'The Livisterio,' 'The Book of Thoth,' The Rauðskinna,' mysterious titles for a mysterious room.

"So many precious things," I said in awe, "a lifetimes collection."

"And yet, another puzzle to solve, look."

William pointed at the floor at our feet. The floor was covered in dust. Apart from our own that led from the door to the bookcase where we stood, there were no footprints in the dust, nothing to suggest this place had been occupied for weeks if not months. William shook his head and let out a quiet laugh that sounded like nerves.

"I don't like the feel of this place Joseph, we should go. I think that the tale of your nightmare has put my nerves on edge, but there is a power here, hidden maybe, but it watches from the shadows."

I looked at him quizzically, to this point he had been full of bravado and common sense. One of the books caught my eye, it was an ancient tome written by Andreas Vesalius. His name was clear in gold leaf along the spine of the book. I reached out to take it from the bookcase but he stayed my hand.

"No. Don't touch anything."

I lowered my hand and looked him in the eyes. Fear stood there.

"What is it you are afraid of? These are just books and the room is bereft of life, nothing here can do us harm. But what else is there to do. If Carter is no longer here, the answer to the mystery of the sword and Edgar's last few days may have left with him."

William walked slowly out of the room and I followed. I was relieved to see that he seemed to immediately relax back to his confident self.

"Would Edgar be familiar with anybody else in Richmond?"

I took a few moments to consider. Edgar had only recently moved back to the city. He hadn't even had a chance to locate a permanent residence in the City. This thought lit a spark of an idea.

"He was boarding at the Swan Tavern. It is close, only a block or two the west."

"Then let us adjourn to this Tavern, he may have left a clue behind in his rooms. If not, I am hungry and we can at least get a bite to eat."

The Swan was only a stone's throw from the office, on the opposite side of Broad Street between eight and ninth. The Tavern was pleasant from the outside, pale red brick with bold red shutters, three stories tall with an open door that beckoned us inside. A long oak bar stood in front of us, a brass foot rail and handrail ran the length of the bar, ornate brass spittoons sporadically placed below. There was a cluster of tables and chairs clustered around the long room. A group of three men were drinking and laughing together at the bar and a handful of diners occupied the tables. The saloon smelled of spirits and barbeque and greasy grilled meat, William was right, if Edgar's room didn't reveal a clue, we would be getting a table here for lunch. The old woman at the bar bid us welcome and we introduced ourselves. She was small, birdlike with a heavily lined face and wizened hands. She listened with patience as I took some time to explain our relationship to her past lodger. When she realized our mutual interest was Edgar, her demeanor changed from charmed and welcoming to concerned and suspicious.

"Mr. Poe disappeared one night, more than a week ago and hasn't been seen since. I liked him but he left his room unpaid," she added, letting the unsaid request hang in the air between us.

"I will settle all of Mr. Poe's accounts…on one condition. Grant us access to his room for an hour."

The key was quickly in my hand and she pointed behind to the stairs that rose to the upper levels.

"Room thirty-two, the corridor to the left at the top."

With that she dismissed us, turning her back to deal with two men who had entered behind us and who had taken a position at the bar to our right. They appeared to be laborers on their lunch break, dressed in heavy boots, rough coats and identical hard felt brown derby hats.

The stairs were steeply pitched and made a turn to the right every six steps. The passage was narrow and the ceiling so low that it forced me to walk awkwardly, my spine bent forward. We passed the second floor corridor and continued on toward the third floor. It was dark and cold in the stairway and the temperature continued to drop as we ascended. The landing at the top of the stairs issued onto a corridor that ran in both directions. Cheap carpet lined the floorboards, the walls covered in a dark green wallcovering design of a foliage in repeating lozenge shapes. We turned left and found Edgar's room half-way along to the left, a room that faced the street. The heavy iron key turned in the lock and the door swung slowly into the room.

The room had been completely destroyed. Not a drawer or cupboard was intact, clothes were strewn across the floor, sheets and pillows had been shredded and hung in tatters from the smashed furniture. Edgar's belongings had been rudely emptied from cases and boxes, upended on the floor, even the carpets had been lifted from the floors and random floorboards raised. We took a few minutes to pore through the remnants of his life but somebody had been too thorough, if there was ever a clue here it had long gone. William joined me by the window and we looked out onto Broad Street below, the folks of the city went about their business. I turned to ask him if he had any ideas of what our next action should be, and for the first time on the closed bedroom door behind us we saw the pentagram, drawn crudely, its five points described the head of a goat, the letters between the five points, horns, ears and bearded chin spelled out SA MA EL LIL ITH. The black paint used to create the icon had dripped fluidly down the door and pooled, a coagulated dark stain on the carpet beneath.

There was a sudden noise in the corridor outside, a heavy footstep. I motioned William to silence and moved soundlessly to the door. I stood listening for what seemed an age but nothing further could be heard. William motioned me out of the way and eased the door open, he leant his head out the door and looked up and down the corridor; seeing nothing, he turned back to me, a confused expression, shook his head and stepped into the corridor. There was an immediate commotion, a struggle and a muffled shout. I rushed to his aid in time to see a hessian gunny sack over William's head and a single assailant with a brutal cudgel raised to strike. I stepped forward to assist, my right hand reaching for the swordstick, when in my peripheral vision I saw a figure appear from my right, a brown derby hat tilted to a shadow over a broad brow and glinting pale eye. A brawny arm, steel grabbed my right arm, my vision was blinded by rough hessian, I had time for one desperate cry and then blackness.

# *Chapter VIII*

*And so faintly you came tapping, tapping at my chamber door,*
*That I scarce was sure I heard you"—here I opened wide the door;—*
*Darkness there and nothing more.*

John Moran sipped a hot tea in his study. The Doctor was poring over a new medical research paper, a treatise on the symptoms and treatment of consumption, or tuberculosis as it was now being termed by the author of the paper, Johann Schönlein, a preeminent German professor of medicine,. Dusk was falling across the windows of the darkening study and he paused in his work to yawn and remove his spectacles. He rose from his chair to turn on and light the ornate gas lamp on the wall behind him. The lamp was forged in the form of a winged mermaid. She held the sconce out before her, a pillar to secure the shade. John had never liked the light, he could never understand why a mermaid would be winged, but his wife Alice had picked it out when they bought the house together so he tolerated it. The light, initially green and faint, grew to a bright yellow and the intricately cut glass shade illuminated the room with shifting sparkles, scattered light across the wall and the contents of the solid and simple oak desk. The desk was cluttered, heavy with papers and books, Moran had been intently writing notes on his research into his brown leather ledger, his favorite ivory Esterbrook nib pen rested beside the ink well.

Medical research had been the mission of his life, and since Alice's passing, thirty years prior, finding a cure or treatment for tuberculosis infection in patients had become his life's work. A just and fitting goal, it consumed his hours, days, weeks and years in much the same way that the disease consumed the flesh of those it infected. A fitting goal, yet unresolved to date. Walking in Patterson Park one sunny Sunday morning after chapel, his beloved Alice had stopped with a cough, surprised, to wipe frothy blood streaked sputum from her mouth and folded slowly to the cobbled pavement. Within six months he was a widower. His research, as always, brought her fondly to mind. They had made a cozy home in this comfortable, if somewhat squat, three story brick house on Congress Court, three walkable blocks from his work at the hospital. They had been childless but happy, content with each other, looking forward to long days and loving nights to sweep them unstoppably toward their mutual old age.

Still alone, and now old alone, he sighed deeply and raked his short fingers through his long grey beard. A single tear tried to form in the corner of his eye but he wiped it brusquely away, he had to be back at the hospital within the hour, and so began to clean the nib of the pen and close his books, still lost, adrift in his memories. Normally a person of light spirits and good humor he had been feeling morose recently, out of sorts and not himself, with nothing in particular to attribute the feelings too.

A faint, irregular tapping at the window startled him from his reverie. The window, wrought iron casement with horizontal saddle bars and diamond leaded lights, had darkened now from the night that had crept relentlessly across the city. He rose and walked confidently to the window to grasp the spiral iron handle to open the window, certain to find a branch from his neat garden gone astray. He grasped the handle to turn when something heavy crashed loudly and with great violence against the casement, so heavy it shook the frame and cracked a pane. Moran stepped back in surprise and sudden fear. Never a man to be easily intimidated, especially within his own house, he grabbed his walking stick, a twisted hawthorn shaft topped with a heavy silver pommel, and stormed out through his front door and into the garden. Rounding the corner of the garden to the window outside his study, he was ready for a confrontation, but there was nothing to be found, no footprints or other evidence of an intruder. Below the window was a sharp sliver of glass, dislodged from the diamond pane by the collision. Moran bent down to pick it up. The old beech tree close to the house, autumn bare at this late stage of the year rustled and a movement drew his stare. A huge raven was sitting in the branches staring back. Its iridescent plumage reflected the faint sickle moonlight, the feathers plump and pointed around its thick neck, a huge chisel hooked beak set amidst intelligent, piercing yellow iris's. Moran stared at the bird and the bird stared fearlessly back. The raven hopped heavily to a creaking branch, came closer and let out a loud rasping aggressive "craaawww" that startled Moran into hurling the glass shard at the obstinate corvid. The bird was not intimidated and hopped to an even closer branch, high but only feet away. Up close the bird was enormous, and if the bird wasn't intimidated, he was. He felt suddenly panicked and short of breath. Without thought he instinctively heaved his heavy walking stick in the bird's direction. The cane flipped end over end as it flew, clattered noisily through the branches and sent the raven finally into the sky, flapping its huge span of ebony wings against the night sky. It let out a final cry in Moran's direction and disappeared into the darkness.

Moran was panting, breathless, cold sweats broke across his brow and a dull ache throbbed in his jawbone. He took several minutes to calm his nerves and slow his heart before he retrieved his stick, still glancing occasionally and nervously into the night sky. There was no sight or sound of the bird, the garden was quiet and neat as it should be. He prided himself on his strength and vigor, he had proven himself able to fend for himself on all occasions but the fright had left him for once uncertain. Regardless, the hospital and his patients needed him and the hour was getting close to the start of the night shift. He shook off the fear and doubt and returned to his house, doused the gas light and retrieved his worn and creased brown leather medical bag. He left the house, double checked the locks on the door behind him, bunched the muscles in his shoulders and began to walk, chin resolute, bristling his long beard before him, heavy determined steps, and this night, unusually, carrying his silver topped walking stick, fist clenched around the hawthorn shaft, club like in his left hand.

The walk through the dark cold city streets, North along Broadway, was uneventful, although he couldn't shake the feeling that eyes had tracked his progress from every shrouded alleyway and veiled passage. His melancholy had accompanied him to his work, it elicited remarks of concern from the day shift physicians who he checked patient notes with, before they departed. Moran did his best to dispel their concern with some strained humor and turned at once to his work. Regular treatments were administered throughout the day, so the night shift was typically constrained to monitoring the condition of critical patients, and the occasional emergency admission. He preferred the night shifts for their solitude and tranquility, and the opportunity to continue with his beloved research.

Before heading to the office, his routine was to first walk the rooms, a final check and execution of his duties before he could brew his tea and open his books. The Washington College hospital was new, a proud addition, gifted to the citizens by the prospering City of Baltimore. It was composed of five departments, the mortuary, a college department where students practiced anatomy and surgery on cadavers, a wing for surgery, empty at this time of day, the general wards, which surrounded the first floor courtyard, and lastly the twenty private rooms on a long corridor on the second floor which was Moran's dominion. The private rooms typically held the chronically ill and dying patients, the care more palliative than therapeutic. He walked the long black and white tiled corridor slowly and noiselessly, opened each door slowly so not to disturb the patients who should be asleep within.

Each patient was as they should be, some sedated and restrained, some sleeping silently, each room identical in layout and furnishing, and lit only lightly by the waning crescent of the moon that filtered through the window.

Moran was half-way through his routine when he noticed a door to one of the patient's rooms open, a wedge shaped chink of moonlight spilled into the corridor. He tilted his head to listen, there was a murmuring sound, faint and low. Still silently, he approached the room, the room of Snodgrass's friend, brought in two nights ago. The patient's notes had stated that when not sedated he was extremely agitated, although no signs of further self-harm had been demonstrated. All therapies had failed to yield any improvement in his mental state and he seemed to be getting weaker and less communicative. As he came closer he could hear more clearly, words being spoken, a rhythmical ebb and flow of sound, a chant or invocation. At the door Moran stopped and peered into the room. There was a tall shape there, a blackness, standing just out of reach of the moonlight, indistinct but seemingly hunched and hooded, rocking slowly backwards and forwards over the bed. It sang an incantation, low, mysterious and threatening. Edgar's body was pulsing, responding, pulled to the rhythm of the sound, his eyes were open, the moon reflected from the pupils, stared back at the shape that leant over him. Edgar didn't appear afraid or perturbed in any way, like the creature that leant over him was familiar to him.

Chills played along his spine and the hairs rose involuntarily along his neck. Despite his fear Moran could watch no longer, he stepped boldly into the room, shouting.

"What in God's good name is going on!" As he shouted Moran hoped his voice didn't betray his terror.

Two yellow eyes turned at once in his direction nailed him to the spot. He was paralyzed for a moment, the shape shifted and roiled within itself, twisted and turned, morphed, changing forms of blackness within darkness. The roiling slowed, the outline of the being slowly acquired a definition and stepped toward him, stepped out of the darkness and into the moonlight. Moran gasped, a sharp breath, "Alice," he whispered, and so it was. She stood before him as he had last seen her, twenty-nine, brown hair falling to her shoulders, her button nose creased with a smile. Time was suspended, Moran raised an arm to reach out to her. His heart pounded and he tried to speak but his throat was constricted, tight with emotion. A tear formed in the corner of his eye. She took another step forward, still smiling and parted her pretty pink mouth. A rush of blood, thick and arterial crimson, poured, unstoppable from her throat, coated the front of the primrose blue shift dress she wore. Blood ran in parallel streams from her nostrils and eyes and she screamed, her voice, high and trill. The apparition disintegrated before his eyes and then she was gone. There was a sudden rush of icy wind and raven black wings that rushed past and through Moran, back through the door behind him and into the empty corridor. A feeling of loathing and dismay simultaneously overwhelmed him and he sank to his knees with a groan. A shadow was in his mind, despair and desperation blinded his eyes, he whispered her name once more and he fell heavily to the floor, his spectacles shattering and scattering across the black and white tiles.

# *Chapter IX*

*Deep into that darkness peering, long I stood there wondering, fearing,*
*Doubting, dreaming dreams no mortal ever dared to dream before;*
*But the silence was unbroken, and the stillness gave no token…*

The room was pitch, a darkness that obliterated all senses. I knew that I was lying face down, my right cheek pressed hard onto wet cobbles. The back of my head was a dull thudding agony. Faint aromas were slowly seeping through the fog of my returning consciousness, old vegetable smells, moldy black wet slime and decay. My hands were tied tightly behind my back restricting my ability to turn but I could hear a low quiet groan to my right. I managed to turn my head to face the direction of the sound causing the thudding pain to double in intensity. I let out a groan of my own.

"Joseph, is that you?"

"Ah, William, thank God you are alive."

"Where are we?"

"A cellar of some sort, but precisely where I know not."

Walker sounded hesitant, like a man waking from a deep sleep, a dream half remembered but still seeping into the present moment.

"What…what happened, I don't seem to be able to recall?"

"We were at the Inn, exploring Edgar's room. We were attacked, followed from Carter's office I guess, and ambushed in the corridor outside the room."

A sound from above startled us to silence. Somebody was coming, a flare of torchlight from above threw flickering yellow and saffron onto the walls, we heard a large iron door squeak open and heavy footsteps descended the stone stairs, came slowly towards us. The faint torchlight granted me my sight and I could see William lying in front of me. He was tied in the same manner, a smear of blood from his head wound stained his collar but otherwise his retinas were responding to the light. Other than a loss of memory, temporary I hoped, no obvious signs of a concussion. My coat had become soaked from the damp floor and my top hat was visible in the corner where it had rolled, battered and creased.

The sounds of footfalls approached, then the heavy, soiled boots of our two assailants were beside us. We were dragged to our feet and before I could cry out in protest a gag was pushed forcibly into my mouth. The thugs frog marched us awkwardly up the stairs. I was uncertain on my feet but, at least in that moment, I was grateful for the supporting strength of the brute beside me.

We were pushed, dragged down a long cedar paneled corridor with doors that led off on either side and finally into a dark windowless library, a vast space with crowded mahogany bookshelves that reached to the ceiling. The room was unlit save the large fireplace on the far wall which burned intensely, logs crackled and spat embers, a blaze of dancing flames created shifting, moving shadows across the spines of the books. There were two high backed chairs by the fire, crafted from elegant oak, detailed marquetry with embroidered gold fabric seating pads. Across to these we were dragged and pushed to sit facing the flames.

We waited in gagged silence for maybe thirty minutes, with no windows to reference it may have been longer, before more footsteps could be heard from the entrance door behind. These steps were softer, not the heavy boots of the derby hat wearing thugs. A man appeared and stood in front of us staring down. He was tall, perhaps only three inches shorter than me, his complexion dark, eyes black and piercing under bushy eyebrows. His mouth was a slit in the dark beard that fell to a point below his chin. He was well dressed, a wool tailcoat fastened around his trim stomach with four brass buttons. Pleated and striped Cossack trousers finished tightly above polished black patent leather boots. He took his time to scrutinize us, walking slowly backwards and forwards before the fireplace. He finally made a decision and nodded to his henchmen, who swiftly removed the gags and cut the bonds that tied our hands uncomfortably behind our backs. My fury had been constrained too long, I began to rise out of the chair, anger readying my tongue to lash venom at our captor but two strong arms compelled me irresistibly and immediately back to my chair.

"Patience please, first allow me to introduce myself gentlemen," his voice was deep and carried a degree of certainty, a man who knew his place in the world, "my name is Doctor John Carter, as I suspect you know, and I would like you to begin with your names and then explain to me how you came to be snooping in my office building and carrying my swordstick?"

I took a deep breath to calm myself. Clearly the two brutes were not to be escaped and Carter would continue to have us restrained until the story was told, so I decided that compliance might be the fastest manner in which to regain our dignity and achieve our freedom.

"Very well," I sighed, "my name is Doctor Joseph Snodgrass, I am a surgeon at the Washington College Hospital, and this," I motioned toward my good friend, "is William Walker a retired Army Captain also from Baltimore."

I proceeded to tell him the tale of how our friend had gone missing after meeting me for dinner, where I had first taken sight of the cane in his possession, how he had left Richmond on the night boat to Baltimore, where he was discovered by chance, by William, who had found him outside a tavern five nights later still carrying the cane.

"And the name of your friend who you saw with the cane here in Richmond?'

"Edgar Allen Poe." I replied curtly. The recitation of the tale had taken some time, my head hurt from the blow that laid me out and I was both hungry and thirsty, unable to say how long it had been since we had eaten breakfast on the steamer.

"Edgar!" he exclaimed, "so he lives still?"

"He does, but for how much longer I am not certain. His physical condition is poor and he lives now in a fugue state, unable to communicate."

Carter's demeanor changed immediately, from captor to host.

"My most sincere apologies gentlemen, I have many enemies, and when my men were alerted to your presence in my building, and in possession of my precious swordstick no less, I had substantial reason to assume the worst, poor Edgar taken prisoner or worse, killed, and with two armed men now seeking my location intent on evil deeds."

"We came only to seek a meeting with you after we found your name inscribed on the blade. We have a mystery to solve to try and help our friend."

"I promise to give you all the answers you need. But first, let me make amends from the tribulation I have imposed on you both."

With that we were escorted to two separate bedrooms on the floor above, fresh clothing and a copper tub was provided, filled with piping hot water and a bar of carbolic to hand. I scrubbed the grime of the cellar from my hands and face and carefully soaked and cleansed the wound on my head. Despite the headache, the amount of blood was minimal, it seemed Carter's thugs were well practiced and adept at their art. After bathing and dressing, the clothes fitting passably, I knocked on William's door and took the liberty of examining his head wound and checked him once more for a concussion. He had suffered a harder blow than me but his skull looked to be intact and the blood had already clotted well around the purpling lump on his scalp. We were escorted back down the stairs and into the decadent dining room where food, hot pastries, pork belly and pasta were provided. The pair of us descended on the platters, the clock in the dining room showed two in the afternoon, we had lost a full day since we were attacked at the Inn.

Carter rejoined us in the library. The two high backed wooden chairs had been replaced with three comfortable bottle green leather scroll wingback chesterfields. A low table was situated between the chairs, a bottle of cognac ready to pour into three crystal tumblers. The fire was still roaring in the grate and the difference in our condition and demeanor, now cleansed and well fed, free men, dignity restored, had put both me and William in much better spirits. Willing to understand if not yet to forgive.

Carter poured us each a glass of the cognac, an imported and expensive bottle of Vignoble Vincent. I took a sip and with the combined heat of the spirit and the flames in the hearth I relaxed my bones deep into the rich leather. Carter's dark eyes gleamed in the constantly shifting light of the fire as he leant into our little circle, he stroked and smoothed his beard, pulled down from his mouth to the point below his chin.

"So what can I tell you to help you in your venture?"

"Let us start with how you knew our mutual friend."

"We were introduced at an acquaintances house here in Richmond several months ago, a Mrs. Mackenzie. Edgar was taking a late dinner with the family, themselves old friends I believe, when I arrived to visit and pay my respects. It was immediately clear to me that Edgar was in some peril."

"How? Did he tell you he was in danger."

"He did not. You may know of my reputation as a master of the occult. I perceived it in him. A deep and disturbing darkness from the moment we shook hands."

The extraordinary claim would, only a week ago, have had me standing to leave with a contemptuous rebuttal, but the peculiar events of the last few days and the atmosphere of the room and its company staid my tongue.

William spoke from the shadows, "can you explain the

nature of what disturbed him?"

"I can tell you that it haunted him, he feared for his sanity if not his life. I was lucky enough, that very night to hear Edgar recite two of his poems. The family had requested it and Edgar had willingly agreed." Carter paused to wet his lips, the fire crackled and spat, "he began with Annabel Lee, a poem he had recently completed, a rhyme about the death of a woman so beautiful even the angels show envy. It was well received and I recall that Edgar smiled charmingly, enjoying the acclaim of his patrons. It was then that I felt a change in the room though nobody else saw or felt it as keenly as I. Edgar began to recite the Raven. From a lively mood he lapsed at once into a manner, expression, and tone of voice gloomy and deep solemnity, gazing as if on something invisible to others, something hiding in the shadows of the corner beyond him, and never changing his position until the recitation was concluded." Carter shifted his position, refilled the drinks and stared into the flames.

"It was two weeks later, on a Friday afternoon, the twenty-eighth of September, that he came here to my home requesting assistance. He told me he was being pursued by a spirit, a specter wearing the mantle of a raven. He asked for protection as he had a journey to take."

"A journey? To where? Do you recall?" I ask.

"Oh yes indeed, quite clearly, he was meeting a friend for dinner at Saddlers here in town and then, on my advice catching the evening train to New York."

"That friend was I, but it was to Baltimore he was travelling, on the midnight steam ship."

"Not so. I furnished him with the swordstick for protection and we journeyed together to the railway station by Hansom cab. I saw him board the train and depart with my own eyes."

# *Chapter X*

*And the only word there spoken was the whispered word, "Lenore?"*
*This I whispered, and an echo murmured back the word, "Lenore!"—*
*Merely this and nothing more.*

The crisp clear morning spread light slowly across the room, illuminated the rough-hewn pine storage unit and slipped across the closed eyes of Edgar Allen Poe. The light gradually lifted the veil of darkness from his mind and stirred him to semi-wakefulness. He cracked one swollen eye, grimaced and flinched from the light that blinded him. He considered for a moment that he might be paralyzed, but his thoughts, still scrambled and bewildered, finally crept to the conclusion that he was tied down somehow, tethered, restrained. His mouth was dry and his head ached terribly, a dagger between his eyes. The place was unknown to him but the smell was clinical, carbolic. Edgar tried to lift his head to survey his surroundings, but as he did so a steel rail of pain stabbed across his temple, red stilettos blinded his eyes, drove his head back to the pillow and his mind back to oblivion.

His dreams were random, contradictory and bewildering, he was both pursued and pursuer, quarry and prey; thoughts became shards of an ancestral mirror that shattered, scattered across the bedroom floor of his mind. He was walking alone across a vast field. Snow covered the ploughed furrows and mud weighted his boots to anchor him to the land. The trees that painted the horizon were skeletons, winter bleached white bones reached high into the racing heavy grey clouds overhead. A legion of birds, crows, rooks, ravens stood guard from the frozen hoar frosted branches, keenly marked his ponderous progress, heavy footfall followed by heavy footfall, leant hard into the wind, coat tails snapping silently behind him. The wind howled, screeched across the rutted field. A single gunshot rang out, echoed mournfully across the snowscape. Edgar shivered and the birds took flight as one, a single entity scattered into a myriad pieces, each one a memory, a storytelling, a treachery, a murder. They flew across the sky, dispersed, then re-combined, they flew toward him a conglomeration in his mind.

Images of his dear Virginia swirled across his consciousness, flowing white nightdress, dancing in a glittering ballroom, sitting upright playing the piano, her hair an ebony waterfall down her back. Perennially young, timelessly beautiful, alabaster skin and timid smile from cherry lips, and then collapsed, her flesh consumed from within, eyes that shone, drenching night fevers, her silk nightdress stained in blood.

He was lying prostrate in the gutter outside a tavern in the rain. Wet and cold, something was on his back pinning him, forcing his face into the water that streamed through the dirty gutters, ran into his bruised mouth and choked him. His vision was filled by the cane in his hand, a feeling consumed his subconscious, if he could only free the talismans within the cane there lay freedom. A strong hand grasped his shoulder and pulled him from the water, a face, blue eyes. The man was talking to him, his lips moved but there were no words, all drowned out by a howling wind of insanity and the disturbed cackle of the maniac in his mind.

An ancient church on a rounded heather covered hill, incandescent light from a full moon threw midnight shadows across the rocky landscape and the abyssal depths of the loch at the base of the hill. There was something in the loch, but as his mind touched on the memory, a howling wind blew across the landscape, he closed his eyes against the gritty blast and when he opened them he found himself in a courtyard, outside a tall building staring up at a darkened window above him. He knew with certainty that the building was a hospital, even though he was sure he had never visited its grounds before. He was dizzy, disoriented, but certain that although he was outside looking up, beyond the window lay himself. A pair of eyes appeared at the window, a sick yellow glare and below them a hint of a sneer. His fugue state convinced him that the stare lasted an eternity, a trillion revolutions of the earth, a billion cycles around the sun, the eyes were simultaneously chilling and familiar.

A dusk faded to nighttime, pinned to his bed, his throat was parched, mouth sand filled with thirst. His thoughts fragmented, repetitive dreams and hallucinatory apparitions. Lucidity peered from his haunted memories, "what happened to Joseph, he was here with me," his own words muttered soundlessly. Joseph was absent, but somebody was here in his room that night. Something was leaning over his bed in the darkness, the clean white moonlight that spilled into the room avoided the shape, eschewed its touch. The shape began to chant, unfamiliar words, a cadence that snared his thoughts. The shape rocked, slowly, backwards, forwards over his recumbent form. Familiar unblinking raven eyes, yellow with reflective iris' stared out of the swirling darkness of the form. A shout from the doorway interrupted the chant and the dark malevolence instantly snapped its intent toward the voice. A weight was removed, relief and lightness lifted his thoughts from dark despair and he veered once more toward the abyss he had named solace and sanctuary. A woman's name was called in sadness and dismay, a scream followed by the sound of a heavy body hitting the floor filled the room and pushed his fragile mind towards blackness.

# *Chapter XI*

*Back into the chamber turning, all my soul within me burning,*
*Soon again I heard a tapping somewhat louder than before.*
*"Surely," said I, "surely that is something at my window lattice…*

Carter's butler interrupted the conversation with a polite cough. A small man, plain featured, small neat mustache and overgrown eyebrows. He wore a neat black suit with a bright scarlet tie that perfectly matched his cheeks. He quietly deposited a silver platter of neatly cut club sandwiches, three pieces of toasted bread spread with mayonnaise and filled with chicken, bacon, lettuce and tomato and slipped back into the shadows.

"Thank you Kilmartin," Carter shouted at the butler's retreating back and we paused to feast on the supper and pour more cognac. Carter stood and moved to throw another log from the pile by the hearth onto the dying embers. He retrieved a black fire iron from the stand, the pommel of which was delicately forged into the head of a ram, horns curled back against the shaft of the poker. Hefting the pommel Carter disturbed the embers, allowed oxygen to fan the embers once more into flames.

"I don't understand why he would mislead me," I insisted.

"His mission was a secret one, bestowed on him by me, he had no choice in the matter."

"You mentioned protection, if what he needed protection from was inhuman, I doubt a sword would suffice," offered Walker.

"Agreed," responded Carter, "but this was no ordinary sword." He set his glass down on the table and leant back, "perhaps I should take some time to first explain the history and purpose of my order?"

"I think that would be truly helpful."

"Then first I must swear you both to secrecy, what I am about to reveal is known only to a few, the knowledge is both confidential and dangerous to possess. Do you both concur?"

The windowless library made it difficult to track time, but my guess was that we had been in the library talking for more than an hour, outside where time still marched, evening must have turned to full night by now. The glow and warmth from the fire were most pleasant and as much as the scientist in me wanted to think Carter a fraud, he had a manner of speaking that instilled trust and credibility to his subject. William and I shared a look and then both nodded our assent.

He began slowly, considering perhaps how much of his story it was safe to reveal.

"My order is an ancient one, founded in Scotland two hundred years ago. Its name is the Hermetic Order of the Golden Dawn, formed from three even more ancient sects, it is a secret society devoted to the study and practice of the occult, metaphysics, and paranormal activities. I am the Chief Magus, or master of the organization in the Americas. Our source of power and knowledge is gleaned and contained in the Cipher manuscripts, copies of which you will find in this very library. The Cipher manuscripts themselves are remnants from a source much more ancient, the Egyptian Book of the Dead, a series of one hundred and sixty five spells and incantations used to assist a dead person's journey through the Duat, or underworld as we would call it. Have you heard of the Rosetta Stone?"

Both William and I shook our heads no.

"The Rosetta stone is a granodiorite stele inscribed with three versions of a decree issued by King Ptolemy two hundred years before Christ himself walked the earth. It is a key. The secrets within the Book of the Dead were hidden from us until its discovery thirty years ago. The three versions of the text, demotic, phonetic and hieroglyphic revealed the veiled meanings of the, to that point, indecipherable hieroglyphs within. With the stone and its inscriptions, my order has, at last, been able to unlock the secrets of the book and gain access to the spells and powers contained within."

As Carter spoke I could sense his excitement and passion building. The shelves and books of the library seemed to fade away, slip out of existence. Our entire world shrank down, was reduced to just the three of us clustered tightly around the roaring, flickering, dancing flames in that timeless room. Absolute darkness lay beyond our little circle. Carter leant forward, eyebrows obscuring his dark eyes below.

"Of course knowledge of power is one thing, to become adept at its summoning and control another. My order is a peaceful one, we seek knowledge, its members are dedicated to the advancement of humanity by perfection of the individual on every plane of existence. Like your venerable profession doctor, we seek to do no harm."

An extended silence fell across the room, the silence broken by an ember from the log that spat and cracked, musket shot loud in the silent chamber. Carter looked up, his eyes wide and glassy.

"The spells however are from an ancient world, a realm where harm, torture and immolation were more commonplace. To re-enact their full efficacy and master true dominion, sacrifice is required."

"You don't, you cannot mean…?" I sputtered astounded at the suggestion.

"No Doctor Snodgrass, my order would not stoop to such depths, even in the pursuit of the ultimate power. Human life is a sanctity to us. There were others within our order however, who were not willing to be constrained by such trifles. Our order split, some now tread a darker path. They call themselves 'The Dux de Obscurum'…The Commanders of Darkness. They have become heedless of risk, seeking to seize and capture demons, some to act on their behalf, powerful servants, others as mere thralls to further their ends. They hunt demons, intent on their control to facilitate the realization of their ambition."

"Which is what?" I asked.

"Dominion, control of government and society, to rule the world, they will stop at nothing. In turn, my order has been trying to seize and capture those who act on their behalf. You stumbled upon the treasures behind my office?"

"We did, it is an intriguing collection."

"Merely a trap, a lure for those who seek knowledge of the occult and the power it can grant. I am afraid you two gentlemen were unwittingly caught in its web. The treasures within are varied in nature, and each in its turn calls to an individual in different ways. You could call it a revealing of sorts. A certain book called out to you, did it not Doctor?"

"Yes I suppose it did. Something written by Andreas Vesalius. I thought I had heard of him but couldn't bring him clearly to mind."

"He wrote a rather famous book in 1555, it was called '*De Humani Corporis Fabrica Libri Septem.*' It is strange, is it not Doctor, that of all the treasures in that room, all the books on the shelves, your hand was drawn to one of the earliest books regarding human medicine?"

I nodded, thinking back to the draw it had exerted on my mind, it was indeed curious, the shelves were lined with hundreds of similar looking books. William leant into the circle.

"As fascinating as this story has been, I still don't see a connection to Edgar. Why would he lie to Joseph here and travel to New York, rather than to the business he was committed to in Baltimore?"

Carter poured himself a large shot of cognac and swirled it around his glass, breathed in, savored the fumes from the spirit, firelight reflected in his eyes from the multiple facets of the cut glass tumbler.

"As I said, Edgar came to see me that Friday afternoon.

He was frantic with his tale of being pursued. I sensed the beast was upon him but it was shrouded, secretive, enacting its intent from the secrecy of the shadows it had summoned. I decided upon an invocation, a summoning of the spirit that haunted him. I believed if it's true nature could be revealed, determined, I could control it and perhaps banish it to the afterworld. The swordstick you were carrying was a part of the ritual we carried out, it is a powerful talisman. You have seen the inscriptions it bears, correct?"

"We have, the blade is covered in etchings and symbols," I answered.

"We wondered to the true meaning and nature of the design," added Walker.

"It is not a single design but rather a collection of many different designs. The sword is engraved with the sigils, occult symbols that identify the seventy-two princes of the hierarchy of hell. Only by knowing and speaking the name of a demon can a measure of control be attained over it, the sigils provide the practitioner a form of their names."

He recalled something, a look of excitement crept across his face.

"There is a book, a grimoire called 'The Lesser Key of Solomon' that names each demon and describes their powers, it is in the bookshelf just behind William."

Carter stood and moved to the bookcase. As he stepped outside the firelight he was immediately consumed by the darkness. Carter must have known his collection by touch, or had the eyes of a cat, as he returned quickly with a heavy leather bound book. Yellow parchment pages were unfolded onto the small table by the fire. Carter fetched a candle from the fireplace and we all leant in, intrigued, to see better.

"This grimoire is a later copy of the original, written by Johann Weyer who penned his *Pseudomonarchia Daemonum* in the 16th Century. He was a Dutch occultist and demonologist, famous and exceedingly well respected in his day."

Carter slowly turned the pages, symbols and secret seals were scattered across each ancient, creased and time worn page, all written in a flowing Latin script. Notes had been added, scribbled across the margins, sentences underlined and crude pictograms scrawled in blotted ink strewn across the pages. He turned page after page until he reached a single page with drawings that clearly matched the etchings on the blade. On the blade the sigils all flowed into one another creating the illusion of a single design. On paper, each sigil could be seen as an individual design, clearly marked and defined. Intricate intersecting lines, whorls and coils, vortexes and helixes described and depicted each sigil, every mark defined the nature, potency and power of the demon it represented. Underneath in neat flowing script the name of each sigil, the name of the demon, was given.

"In a typical ritual the name of the demon to be summoned is known and used to invoke its presence. I thought to use the swords nature to instead force the beast to reveal its identity to me."

"In what way?"

"By placing Edgar and the blade together inside a Goetic circle, marked and drawn in salt, a sacred space would be formed, a ring from which no demon could enter and none could escape. I would perform the ritual of evocation summoning the spirit. My belief was that the blade itself would respond in some way to the presence of the demon, constrained within, and then I could speak its name and banish it."

William's kind face was furrowed with concern, "so you trapped Edgar inside with the demon, was that wise?"

"You must understand William, Edgar was already trapped within a magical circle of his own psyche, he could come to no more harm than he was already suffering. The beast could not however be permitted to escape. If it was revealed that it was a less benign being the circle might not be needed, but until that could be ascertained, precautions were required. Not all of the seventy-two princes are benevolent."

"And did this…demon, reveal itself?"

Carter looked away for a moment, but not before I caught a look of dreaded fear in his eyes. He turned back toward us, his face appeared lined and wearier in the dancing light of the candle, and in a tremulous voice answered.

"It did…it did indeed."

# *Chapter XII*

*Let me see, then, what thereat is, and this mystery explore—*
*Let my heart be still a moment and this mystery explore;—*
*'Tis the wind and nothing more!"*

Ephraim Makepeace woke alone in the house he was born in. The house was on the west side of the city, adjacent to the docks on Water Street, where doors were always locked and windows barred. A squat ramshackle mid-terrace dwelling in desperate need of paint and repair, surrounded by others of a similar character. The small unfenced yard was filled with weeds, broken bottles and litter blown in from the neighboring streets and the docks nearby. The room was bare except for a few pots and chipped mugs that lay coffee stained and unwashed in the sink in the corner. Fat noisy flies buzzed around a pile of trash by the door, mouse and rat droppings littered the bare and dusty boards of the room. The room served as kitchen, living space, and at night, when he threw his yellow stained blanket on the cot, his bedroom. The house had become his own after his dear old mother had died of natural decay at the ripe old age of sixty-one. Never the cleanest house on the street, her passing had sealed its fate, marked it doomed for dereliction. Ephraim yawned loudly and idly scratched his scrawny chest, and thought again about his encounter with the stranger in the saloon the day before.

He had called into the saloon on his way home from his shift at the hospital. The night shift had spilled into the day, after the body of Doctor Moran had been discovered, prostrate on the second floor. Ephraim liked the doctor, he was one of the few of the medical staff who didn't treat him with actual contempt. Unlike that tall, unpleasant doctor, Snodgrass, with his bulging eyes and open disdain for anybody not his equal in station. It was good that Moran was alive and recovering in one of the private rooms. He had been found on the floor of Poe's room, his glasses smashed. It was assumed he had suffered a stroke or a heart attack. Poe himself had regressed into unconsciousness the same night. It had taken hours to catch up with the patient records and treatments, and the day shift attending physicians had kept him back to assist. He was happy though for the extra money, and as he made his way back to his little house, the cold air of an October morning blowing in from the docks made him pull the scarf tighter around his thin neck and rub heat into his hands. His walk took him by the "Horse You Came In On Saloon", and as he drew level, fate rang the eleven o'clock grog bell and he walked straight in.

The interior was dark and the floorboards were tacky under his old shoes. He took a seat at the bar, dampening his elbows and looking around while he waited for service. Only a handful of the usual locals were here at this hour, although the bell would be summoning them quickly enough from whatever holes they called home. Stone columns supported red brick arches that separated the bar itself from the dining rooms. A huge oak wagon wheel hung above his head and supported twelve candles, yet unlit, mounted above each of its thick spokes. The barman took his time but finally sloped across, grunted a question and Ephraim ordered a two bit bottle. He took a shot, the brown liquid soothed his sore throat, his protruding Adam's apple bobbed, he swallowed, the spirit revived and warmed as it trickled down his throat. He considered himself a lucky man, not handsome or rich, far from both. But he owned a house and had kept his job for more than nine years. He enjoyed the work at the hospital, it kept his mind occupied and he was more than adept at the tasks. Cleaning and feeding the patients, administering tablets and tinctures, keeping the rooms in order and the sheets and towels supplied. Moran even let him assist with some of the more basic procedures, injections and bandaging mostly, but it perked his interest. Recognizing that, and wanting him to better himself, Moran had even leant him a small red leather bound treatise on basic patient care. He couldn't read but didn't want the doctor to think even less of him, so he took it with thanks and kept it carefully, clean and entirely incongruous with its surroundings on the window ledge by his filthy cot.

As he was sipping his whisky and muddling through his thoughts a man took the bar stool next to him, nudging his elbow as he seated himself.

"Apologies friend," he said, his voice deep, calm and

resonant.

"No harm done."

Ephraim turned to see if he knew the man, the voice wasn't familiar, but that saloon in that part of town didn't see many strangers. The man was tall, even when seated, his face handsome, unlined and clean shaven, thirty years of age at most. His gaze was clear, ebony eyes reflected his own tired gray eyes back at him. His suit was a dark tight wool weave with a gold, intricately embroidered waistcoat beneath, the pattern of which was difficult to discern. The more one looked the less defined the warp and weft of thread became. The man himself exuded a confusing combination of confidence and jeopardy, seemingly friendly on the surface, but intimidation and violence not hidden or suppressed far beneath the veneer of his good looks. His presence in this place was like the book on his window ledge, out of place, discordant with its surroundings.

"I don't believe I know you," croaked Ephraim, a lump in his throat and faint alarm sounding in his subconscious, his right hand moved to the blade he kept, rusty but edged in his pocket.

"You do not," he said holding out a right hand, "I represent a firm of…," he hesitated, seemingly hunting for the correct word and finally settled on…"solicitors."

Ephraim reluctantly released the hilt of the knife to shake the hand, "Ephraim."

"You work at the hospital do you not, a porter I believe?"

Ephraim was taken aback, surprise showed on his face, about to rise and take his bottle home, away from the disguised menace of this stranger. The tall man reached out and placed one implacable hand on his shoulder, anchored him to his chair.

"Relax Ephraim Makepeace, I have a proposal for you. I need access to the hospital, sometimes at what some would term unusual hours, to carry out some business on behalf of a client we are representing."

"Access to the hospital, for what purpose may I ask?"

The tall man smiled, its intent was to reassure but the twisted curve of his mouth unnerved Ephraim even more.

"Nothing untoward Ephraim, on my life, my client has a…an interest in a particular patient. One in your care, a certain Mr. Poe. He wishes me to ensure that Mr. Poe receives only the very best of care at all times."

"Only staff are permitted entry to the hospital during the night hours," began Ephraim but was stopped when the stranger placed two red gold coins on the bar in front of him. The gold was heavily engraved, letters he couldn't spell ran in a flowing cursive script around the circumference.

"A small retainer Ephraim, a token of our certainty that you and you alone are the man to assist us."

Still scratching, perched on the end of his cot in his cold and filthy hovel, vermin rustled in the trash by the draughty door. Ephraim idly dragged a broken fingernail across his bony chest. His mind slipped back to the scene in the saloon, it was like a dream now, unreal and distant, difficult to recall, slipping through his mind, details the grains of sand through an hourglass. The strangers face, clear and defined yesterday, now a mass of moving images in his mind, indistinct and shifting like the yarns in his waistcoat. The eyes he remembered, ebony, almost without pupils, but what was the color of his hair, was he bearded or shaven, what was the name of the company he claimed he represented, he left no calling card. He did remember with certainty that the stranger had been insistent and strangely, dangerously compelling. After offering the retainer he had immediately left the saloon, confident and certain that the contract was sealed, left the gold sitting in the puddle of spilt liquor on the bar.

Ephraim yawned again, he knew he wasn't a particularly good man. Never averse to picking a pocket or taking the odd item, unlikely to be missed, from a patient's locker; he was poor after all and nobody but himself had ever looked out for him. He bent to retrieve his keepsake box kept beneath his bed. It was made of tin and had been his mothers, used for keeping buttons and needle and thread. The lid had been painted, a picture of a city far away, an elegant man in a top hat pedaling a Penny Farthing bicycle in front of the Tower of London. He remembered staring at it as a child, imagining a life in such a city, far away from here. The picture had long faded through constant handling. Only the man's top hat was visible now, it floated over the blurred street and faded background. He opened the lid and peered inside. The two gold coins lay there and beside them the silver amulet on the silver chain he had secretly slipped from around Edgar's neck on the night he was admitted. The amulet was fair to the eye, charming in a way that the coins were disdainful, pure gleaming silver against the blood red gold of the coins.

He weighed the precious items in his greasy palms. In his left, the amulet, shining and pure, and in his right the coins, dirty and redolent of the sinister contract. He sat on his stained blanket on his dirty cot in his filthy ramshackle house, and considered which would prove the strongest, which would ultimately have the largest sway over his mind.

# *Chapter XIII*

*Open here I flung the shutter, when, with many a flirt and flutter,*
*In there stepped a stately Raven of the saintly days of yore;*
*Not the least obeisance made he; not a minute stopped or stayed he…*

Doctor John Moran was sleeping fitfully on the hard bed in the private room of his beloved hospital. The room was next to Edgar's, on the second floor, with an identical window that overlooked the courtyard. After being found collapsed, the medical team had admitted him to his own wing. The private rooms were normally reserved for chronic patients needing palliative care, but Moran's standing and popularity ensured that an exception would be made. The medical staff made him comfortable, and carefully treated and dressed the contusions and bruises around his nose and eyes he had received as a result of his fall. He showed some immediate signs of recovery to which everybody was grateful, and after tests were made, he was diagnosed with Angina Pectoris, assumed to be the result of his long hours, stress and generally poor humors. Consigned to bed rest, he was being monitored carefully throughout the day and night by the medical staff. Universally liked by the team, all were happy to take extra time in their busy days to ensure his comfort.

This night however his sleep was troubled, he moaned softly to himself, he tossed and turned, sweat soaked the thin sheets. Legs twitched, his respiration was fast and labored. Tonight a mare sat on his chest and rode his dreams with him through the night.

He stood alone on the shore gazing out across a burning sea. The ground under his feet was uneven cooling lava, black tormented rock thrown into hideous crags and pools, stone waves and crevices sculpted by the collision, the hissing, steaming confrontation of the ocean's sudden and unrelenting frigid depths thrown against the molten force of the flowing rock. The land behind him piled into the distance, the sky was black with an orange smoke covered sun that spilled feebly through roiling clouds. Lightning lit the sky, it illuminated distant mountains, jagged against the sudden snapshot of light. He tried to walk, to leave this hellscape but he could not. His sleeping mind perceived, understood at a subliminal level, that he was merely dream frozen to this spot. Nevertheless, the waves continued to boom onto the steaming shore that poured slowly, dripped molten into the abyss before him. Far out to sea the ocean was black, but closer to shore the crest of the waves reflected gleaming shifting pools of blue phosphorescence. The conflagration had drawn deep sea creatures to the surface, driven from their subterranean depths by the cooling lava flow that had invaded their kingdom.

There was a shape to his left, indistinct, shrouded in white, a hint of lace but he was unable to turn, it floated in his periphery. A halting, awkward movement to his right alerted his vision. Far up the hill something approached from the land beyond. It was a mess of contorted limbs barely clothed, grey rags hung in tatters across its ruined torso. Moran's gaze was captivated, held by the presence and erratic movement of the creature. It was still a quarter of a mile away, but it closed the distance quickly as it ran, tripped, fell down the scree of boulders that led to the burning shoreline. His feet were leaden, locked to the land, panic played a macabre chilling melody along his spine. He tried to look away, to look to his left, to focus on the lace and flowing petticoat, surely those of his dear Alice, and as he did so, the thrashing, approaching limbs ceased their frenzied movement toward him. The dream state would not permit him to fully turn to see her, only vision to his right was permitted and it was there his gaze was drawn once more. Immediately the form began to thrash, limbs drummed the ground. It was random in its movement, haphazard, but it gained ground quickly, almost to the bottom of the gradient now, it gained the beach, still distant but moving faster.

Moran groaned and trembled, he knew, instinctively, as often happens in dreams, he was caught on the delicate fulcrum of a decision. If he looked away the beast was paralyzed, unable to move. It was his focus, his attention it needed to achieve locomotion, and yet he could not avert his eyes from its unnerving form. His gaze was drawn in the beast's direction. A promise lingered there, a gift not to be lightly spurned. A precious gift but not freely given, a great price to be ultimately paid. He glanced in its direction. Two hundred yards, one hundred, fifty, the thrashing limbs threw sand and gravel high into the air, the face was visible now but the features were vague, shifting, undefined. There was a hint of eyes and nose, animal in nature, closer now, almost upon him he could discern the maw of the creature, fangs febrile biting in anticipation. Moran finally broke his concentration, with inhuman effort of will he slowly turned to his left and she was there, returned from her moldering tomb, Alice, young and pretty once more. She opened her pink mouth and spoke faintly as if from afar.

"You can save me John, take the gift and heal me."

Moran shook his head.

"It is what you have always sought down through these long years…take it please…save me."

Moran was unable to respond, his throat was clogged, dry and too barren for speech. The beast to his right was insistent on his attention, it slung white burning daggers into his mind, blinding him to his sweet Alice, jagged barbed hooks snared his thoughts, dragged his mind to slowly turn. Against every fiber of his being the demands of the creature were a noose around his mind. Unable to resist, he shut his eyes tight against his doom and turned to face the monstrosity. He opened them and the beast immediately flailed into action, leaped and lunged at his face, it slavered and bit, unnatural vitriolic rage that snapped teeth and jaws at his eyes and face.

Moran woke from the nightmare, sitting upright with a scream of terror, a face was staring at him from the darkness and he believed, without doubt that he was still on the burning shoreline, the beast about to savage him, tear him limb from limb. He screamed, threw up his arms and attempted to rise, protect his face from the attack, and the form opposite did the same. It was merely his reflection on the polished steel mirror of the hospital room.

Moran slowly relaxed back onto the bed, panting, his hands trembling, but he knew the dream had flown; he was safe and closed his eyes. He concentrated on steadying his respiration, breathing in through his nose, holding the breath for a six count and then exhaling through his mouth. His racing pulse gradually slowed with each focused breath. The details and the fear slipped away from him, replaced by familiar quiet hospital sounds, and the solid, safe hospital walls around him.

The dream was receding, fading as all dreams finally do, but before it slipped completely away he knew there was a message hidden within. A gift, promised by Alice no less. He sent his mind back, picked carefully around the memory of the beast that tried to tear him apart. He remembered the confrontation with the raven outside his study window and his haunted walk back to the hospital. A hazy memory of a light spilling into the corridor outside Edgar's room. His mind was suddenly pleasantly flooded, filled with memories of Alice. He thought about her everyday but he was ashamed to admit to himself that time had decayed the details of her face, frayed the form of her body, bleached her smile, all slowly vanished from his memory. All at once, without warning she was clear in his mind's eye once more, vivid in detail, her essence, her being clung to him. Her aroma suddenly filled the room, vanilla and rosewater from the Mille Fleurs she wore daily, he could feel the warmth of her smile, see her small white teeth behind pink lips, touch her hair the color of dark coffee as it fell in curls to her shoulders. Her alabaster arms reached out for him, the nightgown brushed against his knees. Instantly, overwhelmingly, he was grief stricken. A loud sob escaped the throat long closed to emotion, shook the chest and shoulders of the heart he had hardened to his loss.

"I accept your gift," he sobbed through great gasps of grief. He hung his head and wept, tears streamed down his bristling cheek.

It seemed that an age passed until he could fully collect himself. He finally wiped his eyes and levered himself carefully down from the iron bed. He had something he had to do. It seemed plain to him in that moment, something not to be questioned, and it had to be done immediately.

He checked the small storage cabinet that was kept in every patient's room and was relieved to see his clothes neatly folded and stacked. His spectacles were in the bedside cabinet but the glass was missing and the frames were bent. With a curse he let them drop to the floor. With pants secured only loosely around his waist, he could find no belt, he pulled his coat around his open hospital gown, and with his bed slippers on his feet he slipped unseen out of the patient's wing, through the darkened and empty vestibule and stepped through the gates of the hospital onto Broadway. The wind was howling from the Patapsco to his left and the lights from the piers were swinging, arcing light high into the sky and then low across the throngs of people waiting to board the steam ships tethered in their moorings. West he headed, up Pratt Street, the muscles in his shoulders bunched, eyes glinting above his long grey beard that streamed far out in front of him. If trouble was waiting for John Moran this night it would be prudent for trouble to seek shelter and wait another night. His short stride took him past Bartlett's foundry, locked and shuttered, the gas lights petered out, the streets darkened. Shops transitioned to offices, offices transitioned to empty buildings and finally to abandoned lots. Rain began to lash him, cold streams from the north that chilled, but he paid scant attention. Moran turned left into Poppleton Street, he swung open the door to the Mount Clare Train Depot. He entered, admitted a shrieking wind and a swirl of dust and litter from the street. He walked up the to the night desk and rang the brass bell repeatedly until a young and sleepy looking night clerk timidly opened the office door and cautiously stuck his pimply face out. The boy looked at his customer aghast. The man stood there, dripping onto the floor in squelching slippers, straggled, angry grey beard above the chest hair that stuck out of a striped hospital gown that was plastered to his chest from the monsoon outside.

"Y…Yes sir, how can I help?"

"I need to send a telegram," boomed Moran, "immediately."

# *Chapter XIV*

*But, with mien of lord or lady, perched above my chamber door—*
*Perched upon a bust of Pallas just above my chamber door—*
*Perched, and sat, and nothing more.*

Carter paused to once more to collect his thoughts. He leant back into the darkness of the chair and teased his beard through his fist, contemplating the next part of the story. His habit of doing so caused me concern, to doubt his story somewhat. It could be that he was simply trying to recall the precise details of this summoning, this evocation as he called it, intent on describing it with accuracy and clarity to us. Or it could be that he was trying to ascertain which version of the truth to tell, which details to leave in the shadows of his mind, kept hidden from us. He sighed heavily, his decision made, truth or deceit, and leant forward into the flicker of the firelight.

"It was in this room that I carefully drew the Goetic circle, six feet in diameter, pouring salt to create the outline from the iron vessel you see on the mantle."

He leafed slowly through the grimoire in the table until he found the page he was seeking. The page was well thumbed, creased and covered in inked notes framing a picture of a rough circle. The picture showed a circumference of a circle formed from the body of a long green snake that had wound its body around itself two and a half times. The head and forked, protruding tongue rested on the north point of the circle, and its pointed tail was to the south. Strange hieroglyphs painted the length of its torso. Within the circle and at the center stood a diamond, painted red, a black swastika sat at each point of the diamond. The diamond itself was surrounded by four pentangles, one at each cardinal point of the compass. Beyond the boundary of the circle were four more pentangles set out at the points north-east, south-east, south-west and north-west. Between the points of each pentagram, groups of letters were evenly spaced SA MA EL LIL ITH.

"Those are the same letters we saw on the back of the door in Edgar's bedroom back at the Swan Tavern!"

William's memory was returning, I smiled to myself, happy that no long term damage seemed to have been done.

"Yes, they name two ancient demons, Samael and Lilith. Samael is also known as the venom or poison of god, the fallen angel, Lucifer, the devil himself."

"And Lilith?"

"A female demon, the first wife of Adam who came before Eve. She was banished from the Garden of Eden for refusing to be subservient to Adam, she became Samael's lover."

"Nonsense!" I exclaimed, "there was only one woman in the Garden of Eden, the bible clearly states the truth of the matter."

"You must read your bible more carefully Doctor Snodgrass. The bible says no such thing. There are two accounts of the first woman and they are difficult to reconcile. Genesis 1:27 states 'God created mankind in his own image, in the image of God he created them; male and female he created them together.' While only a single page away in Genesis 2:22 we have, 'then the Lord God made a woman from the rib he had taken out of the man, and he brought her to the man.' Which is it to be, good Doctor, did God create man and woman together, at the same time, or did he first create Adam and then carve woman from Adam's rib?"

I scoffed at the notion, it seemed like a petty detail, a minor discrepancy, but I admitted, if only to myself, that I had not considered the difference before and only a chapter apart. Carter, frustrated, waved the matter away.

"Regardless," he continued, "the ancients have for millennia believed that Lilith was the woman created at the same time as Adam. When she was banished she became a demon, in league with the devil himself. She has ridden the wings of time, appearing in different forms throughout the ages, bringing death and terror wherever she went. The name Lilith in ancient Hebrew can be translated as night hag, she is the tree spirit of the Mesopotamians, the bird-footed woman of the Babylonians, the demonic jackal of the Greeks, the vampire of Eastern Europe, the succubus of the Arabs. Together the names of Samael and Lilith have long been tokens of power to those who known how to summon and harness them."

The fire had died down to glowing embers once more. Carter paused while William took a turn and rose stiffly from the comfort of the Chesterfield to throw two large knotty logs onto the fire, he prodded at the embers with the ram headed poker until flames snaked and writhed around the wood, consumed the bark in noisy crackling and popping sparks. William returned to his seat, Carter continued.

"With the circle drawn, I had Edgar take his place, knelt facing me, on the diamond center within, the sword held in both hands, the point stabbed and secured into the floorboard between his knees. I remember I nodded at him, a final question of his willingness to begin and without a moment of doubt he eagerly nodded his assent. I began the ceremony, starting slowly, incanting the hidden words, repeating, the rhythm increasing by small measures. An evocation can take much time, the spirits of the demons are often reluctant to show themselves, pulled grudgingly from whatever dark sinister and nefarious activities ordinarily consume their mysterious lives. With Edgar it was different. Almost at once the sword began to vibrate in his hands. Edgar's eyes had closed and he had begun to rock backwards and forwards on his heels. I continued to chant the words of summoning, the blade singing as it resonated to the increasing power within the circle. A cyclone of dust particles and paper within the circle began to form around Edgar's rocking body and the pitch from the sword keened higher and higher. As my chant increased in speed, the cyclone spun faster around him and the sword hummed and keened its song. Edgar seemed oblivious to the noise and maelstrom around him but as I sensed the evocation was at hand, with a final command I spoke, shouted, the summoning names of power, the names written around the pentangles that surrounded him within the circle, "Samael Lilith!"

Carter paused, his eyes wide at the memory.

"What happened," asked William, perched on the edge of his chair, his blue eyes were intent upon Carter, "you said the demon revealed itself, what was it?"

"It was…something, in all my years of practice in the dark arts I had never thought to see. With the final words of summoning Edgar fell forwards, collapsed onto the hilt of the sword that he still held in his hands and now supported the weight of his slumped body. The room was dark, as you see it now."

I looked across at William, he was barely seated, so intent on the story.

"The light from the fire flickered light onto Edgars back, revealed a form that had not been there before. It was the size of a small infant, crouched, huddled, gripping tightly onto its host, yellow fingers, talons, clawed through his wool jacket, securing itself to his body. Its back rose and fell sickeningly against him, a maggot feeding on its prey. I called once more the names of power and demanded that the demon be named. The sword sparked into light, bright to the eye but a nauseous, green glow of putrefaction. The demon scuttled disconcertingly in the light of the sword, shifted its weight on Edgar's back, ensuring its grip. One of the sigils began to focus the light, drawing it from the length of the blade, faint lines lit by the fire of the room and the sickly gleam of the blade, revealed the name of the demon, the name of the succubus feeding on its host. Edgar slowly raised his head from his chest and opened his eyes, a look of pure terror on his poor face, aware now of the beast's slow writhing movement. I spoke the name of the fiery sigil and at the same time Edgar spoke a similar name, 'Raum' said I, 'Rey A-Nall' spoke he. With the demon identified and its name spoken out loud the spell was broken. The light from the sword and the sigil was extinguished like it had never been, the beast on Edgar's back was concealed once more, sheathed in whatever spells of obscurity it had woven and wreathed around itself. Edgar released his grip on the hilt and the sword clattered to the floor, the hilt crossed the threshold of the circle, sealing the end of the ceremony."

Carter reached for his glass and took a large gulp of the cognac. The timeless room had fallen silent. Outside of our little fire lit circle, the darkened bookshelves seemed to encroach. The fire roared and crackled life into the space. Carter shook his head.

"In all my time studying the arts of the necromancy I have never seen a demon like that, so close, so intimately connected to a human, living off his spirit…his very soul."

"What is this Raum, this succubus?"

"Raum is one of the seventy-two princes of the underworld."

He reached once more for the grimoire on the table and flipped back through the pages to find the page that listed the seventy-two sigils. Underneath each sigil lay the name and a description of the nature of the beast in Latin. Carter pointed to the sigil the sword had revealed and traced the words below carefully with his finger as he read.

"*Raum est enim magnum comitem, ille est, videatur in cantaverit, sed cum ea induitur humana figura suis iuxta imperium Domini omni exorcistæ, si furtum fecerit mirum in modum de domo regis, et portat eam num sit assignata, ipse destruit urbes, atque habeat dignitatum despectum et cognoscat praesentia, praeterita et futura moderetur legionibus.*"

As Carter spoke the words, our small world seemed to constrict even more, the darkness encroached from the books behind them, books of lore and strange Magiks, listening and waking to the charms of the words. A wind whistled down the chimney, disturbed embers and fanned the dancing flames, the fire roared intensely, a conflagration in the hearth. With the last word Carter spoke, a sudden icy gust swept down the chimney, blew a cloud of flaming embers and ashes into the room, each cinder a dark wing, black as a raven. The flames roared in answer and then settled back to their steady and reassuring flicker. Carter and I quickly wiped the soot from the table, dowsed the small embers from the pages of the book. William looked across at me, a look of trepidation and unease, but steeled himself and spoke.

"Your learning as a scholar and a doctor have given you an advantage over me, you both speak Latin, but I was a simple soldier, the words mean nothing to me."

"My apologies William, Raum is a Great Earl of Hell, a ruler of thirty legions of demons. He is often depicted as a crow or raven which adopts human form at the demand of the conjurer. A metamorph, a shape changer with great power."

"You said that Edgar called out another name. At the same time that the sword identified his demon, he also spoke?"

"Yes, Rey A-Nall. Rey is a simple corruption of Raum. It was the name given to him by the ancients."

"And A-Nall?"

"I know not, I have studied my books since that night, trying to divine its meaning, so far in frustration," said Carter, leaning back into his chair.

"I know what it means," I said leaning into the light, "my family name is Snodgrass, it comes from the old Celtic for smooth grass, the name of a settlement in the bend of the river Garnock, outside Irvine in Scotland. My mother spoke Celtic and I retained a few words, 'a-nall' would be translated as 'is here'. Edgar spoke once, the day I left him in hospital in Baltimore to come here. It was difficult to hear, his voice was weak but I believed it was a name, it sounded like Reynold. I see now he was trying to tell me Rey a-Nall…Rey is Here. Raum was still there in that room with him."

# *Chapter XV*

*Then this ebony bird beguiling my sad fancy into smiling,*
*By the grave and stern decorum of the countenance it wore…*

"If Raum is still with Edgar in Baltimore it means my associates failed to rid him of the demon. It haunts him still."

"What associates?" asked William.

"The ones I sent him to meet with. In New York, the night he should have travelled to rendezvous in Baltimore with you Doctor."

I shook my head in frustration.

"You sent him alone!" I state accusingly, "why would you do that once you knew that the beast was upon him?"

"He had the sword Doctor, it would be a most potent force against any attacker, of this world…or any other. Besides within a few hours he would be under the protection of the Fox sisters."

"Who are the Fox sisters? And help me, I still don't understand, who or why would anybody want to attack Edgar?" queried Walker, suppressing a yawn.

"Yes, the night is long, dawn beckons and we need some rest before we are ready to confront the perils of a new day, but you raise two excellent points William. Let me make answer and then we will have our respite."

Carter walked to the fire and pulled a cord that presumably rang a bell in the servant's quarters. He returned to his seat, the servant's quarters must have been close to the library, no sooner was he sat than the butler stepped out of the shadows.

"Kilmartin, please bring coffee for me and our guests," spoke Carter, "and a light breakfast, some toasted muffins?" he asked looking at myself and William in turn. We nodded our silent assents and Carter picked up his thread.

"The Fox sisters are of our guild, valued members of

the Golden Dawn. The three sisters live together in New York. Their names are Leah, Margaretta and Catherine. The House they grew up in was reputedly haunted. The story told is that the spirit of a peddler, a man named Charles Rosna was murdered in that house. There were reports of strange voices and footsteps in the corridors and several personal items of the girls went missing. Years later, after the children had moved, the cellar was excavated, human bones were found buried there, the bones of a man surrounded by dolls and hairbrushes. The sisters vouched that the items excavated had belonged to them. Even at a very young age the girls were reputed to already have the gift, the touch, but as they matured they became even more attuned, sensitive to the supernatural. When the eldest child, Leah reached puberty at eleven, she told of an invisible entity that started visiting her. It would follow her from room to room, whispering to her, telling her secrets, asking her to do its bidding. The spirit also whispered its name to her, Leah called it Mister Splitfoot. As each of the other girls also reached puberty Mr. Splitfoot also paid visit and never left."

"Splitfoot, does that carry some meaning?" I asked.

"The devil is often portrayed as a goat, a beast with cloven hoofs, a literal splitfoot."

I nodded understanding, a shiver ran down my spine, the thought of the devil whispering, unknown secret things to these young women was unconscionable to me, but I motioned Carter to continue.

"They moved from house to house as they matured into young women. In every house, hauntings would occur, strange noises, rapping's on the walls, banging floorboards in the attics at night. No natural causes were ever found. Now young women, they each embraced the spirt world and became mediums, gaining some notoriety in New York for holding large public seances.

In more recent years they took to their craft with absolute dedication and utter seriousness, and since the

Dux de Obscurum grew in power, they were forced to distance themselves from the world of man and hide themselves away. The Dux seek them relentlessly, they would convert them to evil if they could and slay them without pause if they could not. To our order they are held in the very highest esteem, true masters of necromancy and demonology. The most powerful wiccans of the modern age. It was to them that I sent Edgar."

"What could they accomplish that you could not?"

"As I say, they are revered as potent and powerful in our order. I was able to divine the nature of the beast and reveal its name. By speaking its name I should have been able to summon some control over its nature but I admit, I could not. My hope was that the sisters could come to understand how it had taken possession of Edgar, and through that knowledge uncover a way to banish it from this astral plane, return it once more to the underworld.

"To your other question William, I can make answer also. It was discovered through one of my sources that the Dux de Obscurum had somehow been made aware that Edgar was haunted by a demon. Their mission, as I say, is to ensnare and make prisoners of any demons they can locate. They hunt for them across the world, and a secret but incredibly puissant cabal operates here in the Union. Once word escaped that Edgar could possibly lead them to a demon, he himself became prey to their deeds. The cabal had become interested in which demon was tormenting poor Edgar. If they were to ever find out that the demon that sits upon his back, feeding on the poor man's spirit and lifeblood, is the Great Earl of Hell, Raum himself, they would stop at nothing to take possession of the beast. Edgar's life would be forfeit, meaningless to them."

While he finished his story the butler tidied the small table, placed the grimoire reverently back on the bookshelf behind William. When he returned, he poured coffee and used a pair of silver tongs to place a single buttered muffin onto each of three small plates. With the butler gone, we each took some time to enjoy the breakfast, I inhaled the chicory essence of the steaming coffee, savored it and let it revive my spirits, fatigued through the dark night and the long telling of the tale.

"So what now?" I asked, somewhat wearily.

"These Fox sisters intrigue me," said William, "if Edgar made it to New York, they may have information that would be critical to our finding out what happened during the missing five days."

"Agreed, but I am also worried about Edgar's condition, I think we should return to Baltimore." The room fell silent as we each picked at the options, finally I spoke, "what is your counsel Doctor Carter?"

Carter looked concerned, deliberated the choices in front of us. He stroked his dark beard, disheveled at this hour, teased it into the more familiar point below his chin. Finally, he made a decision.

"Hard choices lay ahead of us. I would defer making them until we have had some rest. Even with your best intentions, regardless of your destination, be it New York or a return to Baltimore, no transport will be available until midday tomorrow at the earliest. I counsel we sleep for a few hours and meet again in the morning. Better guidance may be given under the light of a new sky."

# *Chapter XVI*

*"Though thy crest be shorn and shaven, thou," I said, "art sure no craven,*
*Ghastly grim and ancient Raven wandering from the Nightly shore—*

I took myself at once off to the bedroom Carter had prepared for me. The curtains were heavy and blocked out the rising sun. The bed was large and comfortable and after loosening my shirt and stretching my limbs I fell at once into a thankfully dreamless sleep. I woke to an urgent knocking on the door. Checking the hour on the bedside clock revealed I had slept for only four hours but I felt pleasantly refreshed, my head clear as I walked to open the door, buttoning my shirt. One of Carter's henchmen was standing waiting stolidly for me. There was no emotion in his eyes, but in an accent I took to be Eastern European he asked for my immediate attendance in the dining room. I quickly splashed my face and eyes in the bathroom and dressed and made my way hurriedly downstairs, wondering what news was so urgent my sleep needed to be interrupted.

The dining room was already noisy with the sound of knives on plates and cups making saucers ring. There was a buffet breakfast or perhaps it was lunch. Neither my head nor my stomach could tell which, but there were eggs and Italian sausage, bread rolls, kippers and blue cheeses. Coffee pots were balanced on trivets that protected the mirrored surface of the rosewood inlaid mahogany table. William and Carter were already seated, looking tired and bedraggled, also dragged from their sleep. Curiously, the two henchmen were also seated, dining as guests on the opposite side of the table. I took a plate and piled on eggs and sausages and sat beside William, ground pepper onto my plate and poured myself a cup of coffee. My stomach grumbled in appreciation and I closed my eyes for a full minute, shut out the noise of the dining room, enjoyed the aromas of the grilled meat and the black coffee, the sense of safety, peace and solitude that is often most acute in the moments before it must be broken and the next steps, unknown steps, perhaps toward danger, must be taken.

With us all gathered and seated, Carter broke the silence and I opened my eyes in anticipation of the news.

"I am afraid that while we slept, events gentlemen, overtook us rather. Last night Kilmartin, my butler, disappeared."

"He was abducted?" I asked, but Carter avoided my gaze, averted his eyes

"We don't really know. All I can say is that he is missing and cannot be found. I am afraid that he has either been captured or his allegiances have been compromised. Either way, we should assume that his attackers now possess the knowledge of the identity of Edgar's demon. My associates have scoured the city, he is nowhere to be found."

Carter looked across the table toward his henchmen. Realizing we had not been introduced to his associates, and our opinion of them would still be colored by the nature of our first meeting, he paused to correct his omission.

"Apologies Doctor Snodgrass, Captain Walker, let me first take a moment and properly introduce you to my colleagues, please meet Mr. Volk and Mr. Darko."

For the first time I properly took stock of the two men who had attacked and abducted us. They were close to identical in features and build, certainly brothers and perhaps even birth twins. Each had broad, Slavic or possibly Dinaric features, heavy brows, snubbed noses and fleshy lips. Their hands were rudely placed flat on the table in front of their empty plates. Each burly hand a mountain range of bruised knuckles and calcified lumps from breaks and fractures of phalanx and metacarpals. Volk and Darko returned my stare, the eyes were ghostly, almost colorless, staring back across the table without emotion.

The two men nodded almost imperceptibly in our

direction. I chose, at least for the moment to not acknowledge the motion.

Forthright as ever William asked, "what is the nature of your relationship with Doctor Carter?"

Darko sent a dark stare in William's direction but there was no answer from the men and Carter spoke awkwardly and quickly into the silence.

"Volk and Darko are men of few words but they have been trusted companions of mine for many years. Their loyalty is without question and they both possess a certain acumen for," he paused, and I would swear the next word on his lips would be 'violence' or 'murder,' "…protection," he finally continued.

"Unfortunately, the news doesn't get better. Although Kilmartin was found missing, in his quarters a telegram was found."

Carter carefully opened the telegram.

"The telegram is from Doctor John Moran. You know him yes?"

"I do, what does it say?"

"It says that Edgar is at deaths door and that you, Doctor Snodgrass, should return forthwith."

"Nothing more?"

"Nothing," he said handing me the telegram.

I read it slowly, out loud so William could hear, the expense of the telegram service had forced a brevity of words on the sender.

"Edgar dying stop. Snodgrass must return immediately stop." I placed the telegram back on the table and looked up. "The message of the telegram is both urgent and clear I must depart for Baltimore immediately."

"Wait, good Doctor, a little patience please," said Carter, "last night you asked for my counsel, and this morning I promised to provide it. For what it is worth here it is. You Doctor Snodgrass, and you William Walker should continue your journey. Leave as soon as possible for New York, meet with the Fox sisters at this address," he said, as he retrieved a slip of folded paper from his waistcoat pocket and pushed it across the table in my direction. William leant in and took the note, and in turn secured the paper in his waistcoat pocket. He sent a smile, a gesture of assurance toward me and patted the pocket, close to his heart.

"But what about Edgar, the telegram specifically requested my return. I cannot abandon him alone and without a friend in his darkest hour."

"I myself will travel to Baltimore tonight. If the cabal have found out from a source within my own house that Raum is with Edgar, I feel entirely responsible for his safety and will do everything within my power to offer him protection."

"Will the sisters be willing to meet with us, how will they know who we represent?" asked William.

"You will carry a talisman of power and goodwill they will recognize. With this in your possession, the closed door to their home will be opened."

He gestured to the door behind him, propped up by the door frame was the Malacca cane, its secret blade hidden from view.

"When I leave for Baltimore this evening, Volk will accompany me. It would ease my mind, and my conscience, if you would allow Darko to accompany you to New York?"

"Out of the question." I retorted. "I will not allow it. With me and William and the swordstick we are more than ably protected."

"I thought that might be your decision," Carter said sadly, resignation in his voice as he placed his knife and fork down on his plate and wiped his mouth with a cotton napkin. "In which case, there is no more time to waste, a hansom cab is outside waiting to take you to the Clock Tower railway station on Main Street, your train leaves in an hour."

I immediately returned upstairs to collect my bag and

coat and then hastened back downstairs to meet Carter and William at the door. Carter was solemn at our departure, the adventure had taken a dark turn and our journey to New York, and his to Baltimore, had the edge of urgency, time and events beginning to spiral beyond our control. The cab was waiting as he said, a midnight black mare stomped at our arrival in the frigid air of the early afternoon. A harsh wind was blowing in from the North Atlantic, high stratus clouds threatened snow. We shook hands with Carter and he wished us well and promised to travel with haste to protect Edgar, and that we would all rendezvous in Baltimore in a day or two. He handed me the familiar silver topped Malacca cane and we climbed a single creaking step into the cab. The Hansom set off with a crack of leather and a whinny. Looking back I could still see Carter, flanked now by the broad silhouettes of Volk and Darko, eyes shadowed by the brims of their dark brown derby's tracking our progress away from their master's house.

The train station was chaotic. Cabs were queuing to gain access to the curbside, horses nervously stamped and jostled, sweated and steamed in the gelid air amidst crowds of people who swarmed around the ornate entrance vestibule. Amid the towering gothic spires and red tiled roof, the clock tower announced the time as two in the afternoon, thirty minutes until our train departed. I grabbed the cane and my bag and headed towards the entrance. William suddenly grabbed my shoulder and told me he had an errand to run. Without further explanation he disappeared into the throng, shouted over his shoulder for me to buy the tickets and that he would see me in the first class carriage. We were immediately separated by the milling mass of bodies. Left with no other choice I headed toward the platform for the overnight steam train to New York. I booked two first class sleepers, stowed the cane under the flimsy mattress and placed my carpet bag in the overhead storage locker in my sleeper compartment. I locked the door and made my way out of the sleeper carriage to take my seat in the first class cabin. I spent my time anxiously watching the minutes pass and stared with forehead pressed hard against the window to better allow one eye to see down the long line of carriages for William's arrival.

My anxiety peaked, when at two thirty I saw the station master walk out onto the platform and blow his whistle. The guards stepped down from the carriages and signaled that the train was ready with green flags that fluttered along the length of the train. I immediately felt the couplings jar, jangling as the slack was taken up by the power of the tender at the front. Steam billowed, black from the smokestack, filled the brick roofed canopy of the station. For a moment the platform was obscured by the fumes and cinders and then the train was rolling, slowly gaining momentum, the air finally clearing as the stack at the front broke free from the confines of the station. My heart sank, the platform was empty and the train was accelerating hard, quickly passing the smoke blackened backs of the city's houses that jutted up against the railway lines.

I sat back in my seat, despondent, feeling lost, plunged once more into solitude and loneliness. William's company had become dear to me, I hadn't felt this close to another person in many years and it seemed that now he had gone, bereft when perhaps I would need him the most. My thoughts slipped seamlessly into their more familiar melancholy and I began to wonder, darkly, if Walker had simply abandoned me, fearful maybe of what lay ahead. I believed I had misjudged the nature of our friendship and the bond I thought existed between us. I thought back to Carter's refused offer of Darko's company and protection, and now I regretted the decision. Small wet snowflakes were swirling across the world beyond the cold window, my heart was starting to feel as bleak as that late fall afternoon when the carriage doors opened, admitted a blast of frigid air and a deafening rattle of tracks. He was stood in the doorway, grinning like a fool, out of breath, blue eyes streaming and cheeks red from the exertion and the frost in the air.

"That was too close for comfort," he gasped as he threw himself into the seat opposite me. He swept his blond hair back across his eyes, mindful to cover the scar on his parting. His spectacles had steamed up in the sudden warmth of the carriage and he removed them and wiped them carefully on a sleeve. I had to collect myself, careful not to betray the raw emotion, to conceal the anger…dejection…grief almost, from my voice.

"What was so urgent, you would risk missing the train for William."

My voice, thankfully, didn't betray me, he seemed oblivious to the dismay his departure had wrought. He settled the spectacles back on his nose and reached both hands into his pockets below the edge of the table.

"These," he stated drawing his hands from his pockets he laid two double barreled Derringer pistols on to the small table that separated us.

# *Chapter XVII*

*Tell me what thy lordly name is on the Night's Plutonian shore!"*
*Quoth the Raven "Nevermore."*

The train rattled and shook its way through the built up urban areas of the city, the sleet driving horizontally across the windows of the cozy carriage. As we passed the last of the city limits and white fields began to replace the stone and brick, I looked across at William, still catching his breath and rubbing frozen fingers back to life. My relief at seeing him again was palpable to me, although I was intent on remaining cold and professional to his face, the scare he had caused me difficult to shake.

"It was Carter's offer of taking that Darko fellow with us to New York that sparked the thought. If Carter believed the danger warranted that level of protection, I thought suddenly, during the cab ride that we might indeed require some."

"Derringers?"

"Yes, two shots each and a large caliber bullet, enough to stop any man…or beast," he grinned and I couldn't help but smile back, "and small enough to conceal in an ordinary pocket."

He looked around to make sure we were not observed and slid one of the pistols across to me. I tested its weight and balance, and despite never having held a firearm before, it felt comfortable and easy in my hand. The carriage door swung open and I quickly moved the gun to my pocket as the first class steward stepped inside.

"Can I get you gentlemen any refreshments? Coffees or spirits perhaps?"

We ordered two whiskies and reserved a table in the dining car for dinner at seven. The steward moved on, busy with the rest of the first class guests.

"The train arrives in Jersey tomorrow at eleven. A ferry will take us to Castle Garden by noon, do we try and meet with the Fox sisters directly?" William asked.

"Yes, I feel our time is short, Edgar is dying and I feel the need to be with him at the end. What was the address that Carter gave to you?"

William reached into his waistcoat and retrieved the note, unfolded it carefully and placed it on the table in front of me. The writing was erratic, barely legible. I read it out loud carefully tracing the words with my finger as I spoke.

"Third floor, fifty-seven Stone Street New York."

"Good, walking distance to where the ferry will dock, close to Battery Park. I seem to recall that Stone Street is a street full of stores and lofts used by the merchants and importers, not an auspicious address for three of the ages most powerful witches," mocked William.

"Nonetheless, I feel this meeting might be our last chance to discover the truth of Edgar's missing days, and how he ended up crazed and lost outside Gunners."

William made no reply, he stared instead out of the window, at the fading light and the sleet and snow that whipped across the bleak fields, wondering perhaps why he had volunteered for this dangerous, profitless venture. The carriage had fallen silent, we were both in a hushed mood, morose and introspective, lulled by the rhythmic rumbles and shakes of the train as it made its way through the tumbling hills. It rattled over bridges and threaded through long smoke filled tunnels, through silent deserted and darkened towns as we made our way towards our meeting. The silence was finally broken by the train's long mournful whistle, punctuated by the steward stepping noisily into the carriage to announce Washington was approaching, our first stop.

There was the usual hubbub as passengers destined for the Nation's Capital grabbed bags and clothing from the racks above. With screeching brakes and lurching carriages the train stopped, panting at its temporary rest and the carriage partly emptied. The carriage slowly refilled with new passengers, cold, stomping feet, shedding gloves and hats as they found their seats, and then the train gasped its weary way back out of the glow of the city and once more into the sleeping city suburbs and the long iron bridge over the slow inky Potomac. Thirty minutes later the steward announced that dinner was served and William and I swapped our seats for two in the chandelier hung, white linen tablecloth splendor of the dining car. Dinner was magnificent, I ordered the braised duck Cumberland, extremely rare with potato dumplings and William had the lobster Americaine. There were sides of chicken salad, salmis prairie chicken, oyster patties and rice croquette and we ate like Kings, or perhaps more truly, in silence like the condemned, wondering what the dawn would bring. Our conversation was stilted, each deep in his own thoughts, the memory of the excitement of the night boat to Richmond tempered by the violence and revelations of the time spent with Carter. Once dinner was done we each retired to the sleeping carriage and the comfort and welcome solitude of the sleeping compartments.

I woke to the tilt and screech of the train as it slowed to navigate a tight turn and guessed that we might be approaching Jersey. I opened the window covering to reveal a world covered in white. The snow had thankfully stopped but the light was blinding. The train tracks were turning through an industrial landscape close to the Hudson. Cranes and construction sullied the view. I dressed quickly and washed as best I could in the confined space and limited facilities. I had slept late but had benefited enormously, refreshed and eager for the day. I grabbed the cane and my small bag and made my way back to the first class cabin. William was sat waiting for me, a pot of coffee waiting for my arrival.

"I thought I would have to wake you," his smile returned, pouring me a cup, "black, no sugar, correct?"

"Yes, thank you," I took the cup eagerly and sipped, burning my tongue but savoring the warmth and strength it provided.

"We are fifteen minutes I would hazard from Paulus Hook Station in Jersey City. If we are in luck, there should be a ferry waiting for us to take us across to the Liberty Pier."

The train was slowing as we spoke, the rail depot broad on either side now with the Hudson a distant shimmering sliver of water on the horizon. The train whistle blasted across the busy yards, crews shoveling wood into tenders, coupling carriages, readying the steam trains for new departures. A long final sweep of rails took us finally under the glass canopied roof of the Paulus Hook station and the train fitfully lurched to a final halt and blew off steam in a last tuneless announcement of our arrival.

The twin smoke-stacks of the steam ferry New Brunswick could be seen as soon as we walked out of the train station. The ferry was moored, at half steam already, straining against her moorings, eager to depart. Passengers hurried, scurried, dragged cases and baggage from the train to the ferry. As we approached she let out a funereal blast from her twin horns that echoed across the water toward the city. Sailors were already untying heavy water soaked hawsers from the pilings, beginning to release the ship from her moorings. We jogged the last few yards and scuttled across the snow slippery gangplank, just as her bow slipped away from the pier and pointed toward the island of Manhattan only two-thousand yards distant. She rode low in the water, churning the Hudson behind her. The city loomed closer and closer until it dominated the skyline when seventeen minutes later we disembarked.

Liberty Pier jutted darkly out into the Hudson, water stained planks slippery under foot from the nights snow fall. The high snow filled stratus had been replaced by a mackerel sky that arced over the high buildings of downtown Manhattan, portentous of a change from snow to a future rainfall. We set out on foot walking east down Albany toward Trinity Church then right onto Broadway toward Bowling Green Park where once stood a statue of King George III, gone now, torn down in the revolutionary war and melted to make gun shot. We paused there as our destination was only a block or so away. The streets were quiet, just a few tradesmen going about their business. Despite the lack of eavesdroppers William leant in and whispered.

"Put your pistol in your pocket so you can gain access easily if needed."

He was all business, once again the military captain. I shifted the derringer from my left pocket to my right and checked that I could, with the came in my left hand, draw, cock and fire the pistol quickly if needed,. He pointed to my left.

"This is Whitehall Street, the next street off Whitehall will be Stone Street. We should expect an ambush. I will go first, you must follow me on the opposite side of the street no less than ten paces behind, do you understand?"

I nodded assent and wondered, not for the first time, how a surgeon came to be following a cavalryman into such a dangerous place, and now carrying a loaded weapon. William set off immediately, he tipped his top hat over his eyes and strode confidently down Whitehall, I followed timidly in the shadows behind him, hatless and cold since my topper had been destroyed in Carter's cellar. He slowed as he approached the corner with Stone Street and peeked around the corner before walking more furtively into the Street itself. I reached the corner and did the same, not confident in what I was looking for but feeling the need to mimic his more practiced actions. There was nothing that I could see to raise alarm and William was already twenty paces down the street. The street was laid to the cobblestones that gave its name, a narrow dog leg lined in tall brownstone buildings with rusting iron fire escapes that ran the front of each of the building's storeys. I rushed to close the gap between us, checking the buildings for street numbers. There were few on show, but William had stopped outside a ruin of a shopfront a few yards ahead and was surveying the entrance door to the right. He looked back towards me and beckoned me over. I checked the street behind and the windows above him for threats and shadows but all seemed peaceful so I crossed the street and stood at his side.

"This is number fifty-seven, the door is open," he whispered. I could hear and sense the excitement in his voice. I suspected that this was what he wanted when he asked to accompany me on this venture back in the tavern in Baltimore, a thrill of danger, the chance of a fight. I was not ashamed to admit that standing outside that unknown door, the weight of the pistol in my pocket, and God alone knew what waiting inside for us, terrified me. I felt the need to urinate badly and was just about to say so when William grabbed me by the sleeve and dragged me into the dingy corridor.

Filthy uncovered floorboards led into the back of the building, a single door was set off the corridor to our left. A set of stairs to the right led to the upper floors. William cautiously made his way up the staircase, each step one more tread into the darkness that hung above us. We reached the landing of the second floor to find a huge wooden warehouse door hung on sliders. The door was partly open and William looked in, a hand on the grip of the Derringer still concealed in his pocket. I slipped up behind him and peered inside. The vast space was completely empty but light streamed in from plate glass windows along the western wall. Dust motes floated in the sunbeams, danced in the air currents that rose up between the gaps in the ancient, rotted, warped floorboards. William motioned upwards and so we resumed our way once more, step by cautious step up the stairway until we reached a similar landing with a similar door on the third floor. This one was closed, closed and securely locked.

William stepped up and looked for a bell or other

means of summoning the occupants but the door was plain and the walls provided no clues. I took position at the top of the stairs, peering down into the gloom to spy on anybody who might approach from our rear. The stairs behind me proceeded up to the fourth floor but at the top was only blackness. William looked across at me.

"Keep watch carefully Joseph, it seems we will have to knock and announce our presence. Let us hope that in giving away our position we don't draw the attention of something that we would have rather kept ourselves concealed from."

William struck the wooden door, a booming sound reverberated around the hall. No response. He struck once more, but again, once the booming echoes ceased, they were replaced by silence. Frustrated, William started to bang repeatedly against the door. I was as frustrated, to have come all this way when every sense of my being told me I should have been travelling to offer poor Edgar some compassion in his last days. I turned to look once more up the staircase behind me and while William beat in futile anger against the doors I started to climb into the pitch blackness to the fourth floor. Ignoring the repeated boom, boom of the door below, I proceeded slowly step by step, feeling each tread with my toes in the inky darkness, right hand steadying myself against the wall. I was ten steps up peering hard into the gloom, trying to ascertain any object in front of me when I took another step and banged my head hard against the wall in front of me. I shouted for William and he came slowly up behind me, careful too in his procession up the darkened staircase.

"What is it," he whispered.

"The staircase, it doesn't go anywhere, it just ends."

He pushed carefully past me and felt the wall with his hands, there was no door, no side passage, simply a wall built across the stairway.

"A false stairway!" he exclaimed, "there is no fourth floor."

Excited he ran blindly back down to the third floor.

"Joseph, come quickly, help me!"

I descended, a trifle more carefully, and found him on his knees on the third floor landing peering intently at the bottom of the false staircase.

"Look!"

I knelt beside him and looked at what he was pointing at. The bottom step of the false staircase was secured to the ground by a latch. William released the latch and we both grabbed the tread of the bottom step and lifted vertically upwards. The bottom eight steps pivoted upwards from the floor and then folded neatly back on the upper steps, like an attic staircase. A narrow corridor was revealed beneath. The corridor was lit a yellow glow from a source that was difficult to pinpoint. William motioned me to step inside and once in, William followed me and pulled the secret staircase closed behind him. We walked slowly down the corridor, it was clean and well used and lead on for maybe twenty steps. We tiptoed comically down the narrowness of the space, I bent almost double and William's shoulders wedged against the walls until we reached a low door at the end of the corridor. William pushed against the door which was unlocked. It swung open easily to reveal a vast space. A row of tall windows ran the length of the far wall, permitting views across the roofs and chimneys of lower Manhattan. The color of the sky matched that of the Hudson, created the illusion of a vast ocean that spread out in front of us. Three simple chairs were arranged at the very end of the room. On each chair sat a young woman.

"Welcome Joseph, welcome William, we recognize the key you have in your possession as a symbol of friendship, please sit and tell us what it is you seek here."

# *Chapter XVIII*

*Much I marveled this ungainly fowl to hear discourse so plainly,*
*Though its answer little meaning—little relevancy bore…*

I ducked my head to step through the small opening. Rain had begun to fall across Manhattan, streaking the large windows and distorting the buildings on the skyline and quickly sweeping the city of snow. A labyrinth of mirrors was arrayed throughout the space, strategically placed to lead the eye down a dog legged corridor towards the women. The mirrors were mismatched in design, some wood framed and gigantic, other smaller and fixed into frames that allowed them to tilt and pivot. Mismatched and yet strangely apt. They cunningly reflected the light from the windows to create a tunnel of luminescence through which we walked. Our reflections were at once taller and shorter, thinner and broader as we walked between images of ourselves distorted by the intermingling of plain, concave and convex. The three women were seated at the far end of the corridor, illuminated by the afternoon light that spilled weakly through the fast moving clouds beyond the room. The women bore a strikingly close resemblance, all clothed in black taffeta dresses, buttoned high beneath chins, the same jet black hair parted down the center. They shared delicate features, small mouths beset by narrow lips, with serious intelligent dark eyes under graceful brows. The eldest of the sisters was sat in the middle, the other two too close in age to discern. I stepped forward awkwardly holding the cane out toward the eldest of the sisters in supplication.

"It is only ten days since we last beheld this talisman," said the eldest sister, her voice harsh and judgmental, "a second seeing can only augur bad fortune."

The young lady seated to our right raised a hand in protest.

"Forgive the bad manners of my sister, let me at least

introduce ourselves to you. You have travelled too much in too few days to be called harbingers of ruin at the *first meeting*." She spoke kindly, although the manner in which she stressed first meeting, made me conclude that our intent remained open to judgement. "My name is Catherine, Margaretta sits to your left and Leah is the eldest and oftentimes the most censorious of our kind."

Rather than bridle at the insult Leah nodded in affirmation of the truth spoken by her younger sister.

"You speak truly sister, although a raven darkens my thoughts at the sight of this charm, returned once more."

"A raven?" said William approaching the group.

"Not the raven you are thinking about William," said Margaretta, "Leah speaks only of Apollo's messengers, foreshadowers of evil, a bad omen."

"Please," said Leah, "tell us how we can be of service?"

"We came to find out what happened to our friend, the man you met ten days ago, Edgar Allan Poe. Doctor Carter tells us that he sent him to meet you. You recognize the swordstick, which confirms Edgar was here. Please tell me how he was?"

"He was well, somewhat confused and frightened but he was clear in his request for assistance. We fed him and helped him and he left the next day."

"How did you help him? Carter thought that you might be able to find a way to rid him of his…"

"You struggle to say the word Joseph? You don't wish to believe in the existence of the supernatural. I understand your reservations. As a medical Doctor, as a scientist you have been trained in skepticism. You are unwilling to relinquish your beliefs." Leah paused and looked at me intently, her dark eyes narrowed, pupils dilated. I was captive to her gaze. As she stared, it seemed an age passed, the world beyond faded, there was only the connection between me and this strange woman. Her long fingers were softly motioning in her lap, subtle gestures that stirred my thoughts, spider movements in my mind. I could feel her mind probing the edges of my own, looking for a point of entry, testing, searching. I wanted to look away, to break the connection but she was part of me, I was locked to her consciousness. Her fingers formed a circle, long nails tapping, Deathwatch beetle clicks as she knitted her fingers together. My thoughts raced to block her as she touched my psyche but the effort was too much, I was unable to fight her, she was too practiced and I a child. Her lips moved silently, I let out a gasp then all at once she was inside my mind, speaking directly to me subliminally, wordlessly.

"Relax Joseph, I mean you no harm but, Joseph, you must learn to believe. And quickly, the gap that separates the world in which you believe and the realm that transcends nature is narrow. In some places it is a gossamer thread, a diaphanous membrane, easily parted by one who knows how. Your survival will depend upon your ability to believe. You have already stepped across a threshold, one footfall into a world far beyond scientific understanding. Creatures from that domain are looking at you now, hands reaching out to snare your human mind and drag you across the divide. They see you and they disavow their doubt, they see you and they are febrile for your demise, they are famished and only your soul can satiate their hunger. Your survival lies in understanding and learning to divine when those demons are at hand and how to avoid their lures. Believe Joseph, believe or perish."

The connection was gone as quickly as it was established. Leah continued to hold my gaze but her pupils had constricted naturally against the light in the loft, her dancing fingers stilled, laid at peace in her lap. I looked across at William but he seemed oblivious, completely unaware of the hidden conversation.

"Find a way…to rid him of the demon." I finally managed to say, my voice dry and breaking over the final word.

The three sisters all look satisfied that a defense has

been breached, a barrier removed, a silent test has been passed, that now we were ready to proceed. For myself, I felt violated. That somebody could take control of my thoughts so easily, to enter my mind at will. My hands were shaking and my head ached from the failed effort to banish Leah from entry.

Leah stood at once and walked over to me. "Come with me for a moment," she whispered kindly to me. She took my hand and lead me back down toward the corridor of mirrors.

She stood me carefully and precisely between two large antique mirrors that faced each other and reflected our images perfectly. The mirrors were huge, seven feet high and five across, suspended from almost black mahogany frames that allowed them to tilt on hand crafted silver mounts and align with each other perfectly. The frames were intricately carved with the hideous tortured faces of goblins, imps and demons. Inlaid silver filigree outlined their forms and gave them bright eyes. Stars and crescent moons wrapped around the design. As we stepped between the mirrors, an infinity of reflections, of Leah and I, sprang into the distance. My image stood looming tall over that of Leah and as I always did, I looked away from the image of myself that I detested, the lanky limbs and hard protruding eyes that stared back and judged me. Leah didn't seem to notice or care to my appearance and nudged me to look back once more at the reflections. I did so and saw that each reflection was identical but smaller and smaller as the glass bounced light between them, receding for an eternity into the distance.

"All of the mirrors in this room are precious. Hand crafted by artisans in their trade. Coated with Speculum metal, an alloy of copper and tin to create the finest optics, and imported at great expense from India and China. But these two are the most precious, they are what those skilled in their manipulation would call 'Scrying Mirrors,' in the right hands the light they reflect can be used to unveil hidden realms. How many reflections do you think you can see in the mirrors Joseph?"

"An infinity?" I marveled, "they seem to go on forever, each smaller than the last but receding forever into the distance."

"No. Look closer. As each image gets repeated it loses strength, it passes closer to the realm of the supernatural. As it does so, some essence of its being becomes captured by the spirits that reside within that realm and are so lessened. The entities within the realm beyond the glass of the mirror absorb and feed on the lifeblood within the images and they become fainter and darker. There are no more than perhaps a hundred or so reflections, although it may not appear so to you."

I peered intently into the depths of the glass and saw that she was correct. The images did diminish as they disappeared into the distance. Each smaller and fainter, more shrouded in shadows than the last.

"Do you also see how thin the divide is stretched between this world and the next."

For a moment I was puzzled as to what she wanted me to see, but as I stared at our images, I began to realize there was something wrong. As I scoured the farthest images, so small that my eyes ached, I discerned a darkness behind a distant, tiny reflection of myself. I leaned in closer to see better. My reflection also leaned in and revealed a dark and shadowy shape that stood at my shoulder, dark and indistinct, but moving, its face close to my own, almost touching.

"What is it. What do I see?" I whispered, still staring at the dark shape that stood behind me.

"Your death Joseph. The specter of death that journeys everywhere with every one of us. It becomes welded to your lifeforce at the moment of conception. For some, the reflection looms large and near, so close that they perish before they can even escape the womb. For others, the specter appears distant, seventy, eighty, a hundred reflections even, but always moving, unassailably closer as each day draws to a close."

"And my…specter…how far away…"

Leah smiled for the first time, she looked into the reflection and back at my face.

"A long time, days without number I think Joseph."

Catherine had approached while I stared at the approaching entity, she appeared in the mirror at my elbow and spoke, making me jump.

"Perhaps some refreshments before we begin. You need a moment Joseph, come both of you," she said motioning now to William, "follow me, let us make ourselves more comfortable and I will bring some drinks and a little food."

William looked perplexed in my direction. I could see that he had sensed that something had occurred, a secret conversation to which he had been excluded and then the hushed talk between myself and Leah between the mirrors. He understood something had taken place but was unable to divine precisely what.

The sisters beckoned us towards a door at the far end of the lofty space. The room on the other side was small and homely, burgundy satin drapes lined the walls and partly covered a small window that looked out over the cavernous space. A round table was in the center of the room surrounded by tall backed wooden chairs. Behind the chairs, another large mirror was mounted on the wall, this one ancient and so heavily tarnished it only barely reflected our forms as we entered. We sat around the table, séance like, while Catherine busied herself in the small kitchen beyond, returning with tea and sandwiches. She poured the tea from an octagonal pewter teapot into delicate china teacups. I took a sip and wrinkled my nose in distaste.

"Peppermint and Licorice," said Margaretta with a wicked grin that made me smile even as I pushed my cup away. The sandwiches were welcome however, simple cheese and ham, fresh and tasty. There were juicy grapes, bursting with flavor on the plate beside the sandwiches, they slated my thirst better than the tea and I ate more than my share.

The ladies were seated in the same order, Leah in the center, Catherine to her right and Margaretta to her left.

"Where to begin." I started.

"Wait!" Margaretta's face stared in my direction, her eyes never left mine as she searched my eyes divining something hidden there. I was shocked and perplexed when she finally spoke, an accusation.

"Perhaps you should first explain Doctor, how it is that you have already looked into the eyes of the beast yourself and have brought that memory with you to this place?"

# *Chapter XIX*

*For we cannot help agreeing that no living human being*
*Ever yet was blessed with seeing a bird above his chamber door—*

I started to protest that I had no idea what Margaretta was talking about but she held up a hand to stop me.

"Deep green water, strangled by pondweed, the ruins of a church above? And the eyes of the beast rising to consume you. You have seen this have you not Doctor?"

"Yes, I suppose, but only a dream," I objected.

"No!" she shouted, "not a dream. A memory. Think back to that memory, you looked into its eyes. You saw a reflection of a face, yes?"

"Yes, my own, I was screaming."

"Not your own, think again…carefully."

I replayed the end of the nightmare in my mind, concentrated on the fragmented details from the dream I had had only a few mornings ago, when I woke on the paddle steamer, the yellow eyes rising from below, a face reflected in the jaundiced pupils. I had assumed the face was my own, a rictus of fear stretching the features wide. Slowly the memory resolved itself, the vision clarified, reluctantly I forced myself to once more see the eyes, staring, yellow pupils reflective, a face.

"Edgar," I gasped, "the face was not my own, it was Edgar's."

"Truly," spoke Margaretta.

"You say a memory, then what I experienced as a nightmare actually happened to Edgar? How? When?"

"As you know, Edgar came to us, sent by Doctor Carter. Doctor Carter had divined that the demon borne by Edgar was Raum, as revealed at the summoning. Doctor Carter wanted our help to try to understand how Edgar came to be haunted by the beast. To that end we placed Edgar in what you would call a hypnotic trance in this very room."

"You hypnotized him?" said William.

"Not quite. The word hypnotism is…imprecise. I used a word that you would at least have some familiarity with. With us three, things are more complex."

"It is where our true power springs from," interrupted Leah, "I will try and explain. In the domain of witchcraft a witches' power will rise in one of the three theurgies, evocation, divination or necromancy. Once in a thousand years a witch may appear who is adept in two of those theurgies. Never in history has one excelled in all three."

"Until this day," said Catherine.

Leah smiled at her sister and shook her head sadly.

"Not even until this day dear sister," Leah said looking back at us, "it just so happens that we three are adepts at one of each of the three theurgies, and when we work together the three of us become greater than any who came before us. I am an adept of the art of necromancy, the red code that reveals hidden knowledge and the ability to communicate with the world of the dead."

"I am an adept of the art of evocation, the blue code. I have the power to summon and control the spirits of the underworld," said Catherine.

"And I, least of the three,' spoke Margaretta, eliciting amused but kindly looks from her sisters, "am adept at the art of divination, the purple code. I have the power of an empath, able to divine the truth and gain information even from those who refuse to yield it willingly."

Leah continued, "we each could sense that the spirit which he bears has been with him for a very long time. We employed our individual theurgies, but as one, to execute a form of age regression, taking him slowly back through his years until the demon first showed itself to him."

William leant in, captivated by the tale, "and what did you find?"

"We were correct in our suspicions, Edgar was snared by the demon when he was a boy, perhaps only ten years of age."

"He would have been in England at that time." I said.

"In Scotland actually," said Leah, "he was at school in Stirling at the time."

I nodded in agreement with the dates as I knew them. "He returned with his family to the United Colonies when he was eleven, so that would make sense to me. So what happened, did you find out where the demon came from?"

"We did, it is a long tale but worth recounting in full I believe," Leah took a sip of tea, sat upright and began.

"The full story goes far, far back in history, to the year 1590. It began when a young man called John Fian, a simple schoolmaster, was arrested for witchcraft. It was a terrible year in the history of Scotland. Witchcraft trials had begun in Denmark and had moved to Scotland soon after. Over seventy people would be put to death for that crime by the end of the year."

"But surely, most of those unfortunates were innocents. The witch hunts were infamous for targeting village gossips, a puritan cleansing of those unable to defend themselves from the accusations and rumors of their neighbors," I protested.

"You speak truly Joseph, but that was not the case with John Fian. He publicly and openly confessed to having a compact with Lucifer, and proved himself a warlock in front of King James himself by taking possession of one of his courtiers. He was arrested and tortured most horribly."

"Tortured? In what way, weren't witches just burnt or thrown in the local mill pond?" asked William.

"Fian was subjected to much worse trials. First his fingernails were forcibly extracted, iron pins were then hammered into the flesh before the 'pilliwinks', finger and thumbscrews were used to crush what remained. Fian is reliably reported as making no noise or showing any signs of pain during his trials. He absolutely refused to renounce the devil. His interrogators progressed to the Spanish Boot to force his renunciation."

"The Boot? I have never heard of such a thing?"

"It is an evil device made from wood or iron which encloses the naked foot. The inside of the boot is filled with iron spikes and sharp burs. A vertical plate behind the sorcerer's heel fits into a grooved track and can be moved slowly forward against the foot by turning a wheel. The steadily increasing pressure first forces the toes against the spikes, mangling the flesh and crushing bones. As the wheel is turned the plate moves ever forward until under inexorable pressure, the bones of the instep eventually give way and the arch of the foot is shattered."

"Good heavens," I said, distraught at the thought of the agony of such a contraption, "and that caused him to renounce his pact?"

"He tried at the last, but here is where I believe we see, for the first time, Edgar's demon appear. Fian did at last try to renounce his satanic pact, but in answer Lucifer spoke to him and told him that he would forever be in league with the devil. To assure the pact was never broken, a great Earl of Hell would be forced upon his soul for all eternity. That demon would present itself in the form of a large Raven, black as night, that would ride his back through the gates of hell."

"Raum," spoke William.

"Yes, we believe that to be the case," said Catherine quietly.

"What happened to Fian?"

He was taken to a final meeting of magistrates at a church outside Stirling, a place called Kirk O'Shotts where he was strangled, his body burnt and thrown into the loch."

Margaretta picked up the story, her voice soft and saddened.

"And there his body lay for nearly three centuries, his soul bonded in fate to that of the demon the devil had condemned him to spend eternity with."

"Until his body was disturbed," said Leah.

"Truly, as you say dear sister. One night some boys,

truants hiding away from school happened upon the Kirk and the black Loch beneath. They held a séance, just children playing, imitating adults. They had a spirit board and in their play they accidently awoke a creature. The precise details here were fragmented, difficult to pinpoint."

Leah interjected to clarify a point, "even within our control this part was difficult to make sense of. Edgar was reluctant to reveal all that occurred that night. There were promises made and secrets sworn and even in his removed state Edgar would not willingly reveal all to us. He was at the séance, we know that much, but he was forced in some way to take part."

"Regardless, we do know that a game was played," continued Margaretta, "the boys asking each in turn to name a desire, a wish to be exchanged for a tribute paid to a spirit if one could be summoned. And we do know that something did appear to them in that dark decrepit church. The boys panicked and ran, Edgar ran with them, over the thick heather and down the hill. He lost his footing and tripped, slid down a wet bank and fell twenty feet into the lock beneath the Kirk."

Leah stood and walked away from the table, her hands clasped in front of her.

"The demon, long frustrated by weary years abiding by its masters command to haunt and torture the soul of Fian, seized the chance at escape. A fresh soul unexpectedly entered its domain, Edgar nearly drowned that night, as you know Doctor, but was saved and at the same time damned by the beast that fell upon him. He has carried it with him ever since."

Silence descended around the table as William and I digested the facts as they had been presented. It was abhorrent to me that the soul of a boy only ten at the time had become bonded to this demon that lived and fed on him, succubus like, hidden for many long years as he had matured. I let out a sigh and finally summoned the strength to ask.

"You mention a wish made in exchange for a tribute paid. Could you divine the nature of such a thing?"

A look of concern passed across Leah's face.

"As we say, Edgar had created a veil in his own mind over the events of the séance. The veil had been long in its making, every second of his life since that event had become a stitch in the fabric that shrouded the truth. That said, Margaretta here, who claims she is the least of us, is in many ways more gifted than us all. She is an empath, a soothsayer of the old order. Employing her gifts she at once had a breakthrough into the true nature of the pact." Leah looked sharply across at Margaretta, who looked pained but continued the tale.

"Great care must be taken to reveal secrets so deeply secreted away. The mind can be disturbed and broken if it is forced to disclose that which it requires to remain secret. I held Edgar's head in my hands and spoke the hidden words that invoke the truth to be told, the '*Probitatis Exponentia*'. He struggled and fought me but slowly, and gently, I secured some measure of the truth. Even as a boy, his dream was to become a writer, published and successful in both renown and fortune."

"So his wish was to become rich and famous? That makes sense to me although he is only now, quite late in life, on the cusp of achieving that wish. His fame has quite literally come to him in the last two years of his life."

Margaretta looked even more disquieted.

"You must remember that when Edgar made the tribute, it was far in the past when he was ten."

Both William and I leant in, hands steadied on the edge of the table.

"Please Margaretta, tell us what you must."

She breathed deeply and looked once at Leah and Catherine. Both ladies returned her gaze and nodded supportively.

"There is no easy way to say this. Edgar promised to the devil...in return for his fortune...the life of his first wife.

# *Chapter XX*

*Bird or beast upon the sculptured bust above his chamber door,*
*With such name as "Nevermore."*

The lights in the small room grew dim as Margaretta finished her tale, the clouds through the windows in the loft space beyond had grown even heavier, the lowest of them now dragged tendrils of cloud across the tops of the buildings of lower Manhattan; a curtain fell across the Hudson completely obscuring the docks of Jersey. I placed my hands together on the tabletop and leant my chin on my chest, resting the weight of my head that seemed heavy with the burden of the revealing. I stepped mentally through the past few years to seek either corroboration, or preferably, a way to refute the tale. Edgar had been slow to achieve any degree of notoriety. Writing for jaded newspapers and unread publications, interspersed by bouts of creativity, his work was universally ignored by any but his few family and friends. I did recall the year Virginia first fell sick, it was the winter of 1842, Edgar had just turned thirty-two. She was playing the piano when she coughed, a globule of blood and mucus, a dark foreboding soiled her lace gown, she was just eighteen. Five short, difficult years later she was dead. And it was undeniable that during those five years Edgar had written and published all of his most successful works, 'The Pit and the Pendulum,' 'The Raven,' 'Murders in the Rue Morgue' and 'The Masque of the Red Death,' all to national acclaim and recognition. I could not deny that the timeline was damning. Still, I had to protest, I knew Edgar, and I was certain that he wouldn't willingly have condemned Virginia to such a fate even for all the fame and money in the world. I looked to William for support but he was distracted, his face turned away, alternately looking out of the small window, then down at his hands.

"But if he knew this marriage would result in the death

of his wife, why would he marry her?"

"That I cannot fully answer Joseph," Margaretta spoke gently, her face full of concern, "he did say one more thing that puzzled us all greatly."

"What…tell me?"

"He was certain he had cheated the devil, found a way for the tribute to remain unpaid. He chuckled as he told us, whispered as to a confidant, 'the marriage was made sanguine and therefore beget in sin. With it so being it passed beyond the reach of the hand of Lucifer,' I am afraid it made little sense to us."

I considered the wording carefully for a moment, it was a strange choice of phrasing.

"Sanguine? Edgar's marriage to Virginia was both cheerful and full of hope, but why would those simple characters of a marriage somehow make it beyond the reach of the devil himself?"

Margaretta shook her head, "truly, we have pondered the phrase for long hours, it means nothing to us."

There was a long silence, deep in thought as we tried to unpick the riddle Edgar had left us with. I ran the peculiar phrasing around my brain to little effect when William who had been distant and unusually distracted during the conversation spoke quietly.

"Is not sanguine a chalk, a red chalk, I used to draw and paint as a child, it seems to ring a bell in my memory?"

I turned to stare at his face but he was still looking down at his hands, I was shocked at my ignorance and stupidity.

"Yes William it is. It is the color of dried blood. Named from the original Latin for blood or bloodline!"

Leah was excited at the revelation but still could not place the pieces of the puzzle in the correct sequence.

"Bloodline, what bearing does that have?"

"Edgar's choice for his first wife was extremely controversial and met with great criticism. His wife Virginia was the daughter of Maria Poe-Clemm, the sister of Edgar's father David; Virginia was Edgar's first cousin, a blood relative, a direct bloodline descendant of their mutual grandmother, Elizabeth Cairns."

The sisters looked to one another and I sensed a hidden conversation was taking place, their eyes were at once without pupil and their fingers made small twitching movements, subtle to be sure, but having witnessed it mentally I could see the shapes they described as they conversed without sound. Finally Leah looked up at us.

"This is new information to us but solves only part of the riddle. If it is true, Edgar believed that marrying into his own bloodline would break the need to pay the tribute. But Virginia died, so what went wrong?"

I hung my head and cursed myself a thousand times, a groan escaped my lips and I banged the table in anger and frustration.

"Joseph, what is it, what do you know."

I leant back making my chair creak under the shifting weight.

"When they married and the controversy finally hit the newspapers, Virginia was only a girl at the time of their marriage, barely thirteen. A marriage between a man of twenty-seven and a young girl who was his first cousin. I thought I could help, I visited Elizabeth Cairns in Baltimore where the family grew up; it was a tiny but meticulously kept house in Mechanics Row. I thought if I discovered the facts, as a somewhat respected medical Doctor I might find a way to better reframe the controversy and put the matter finally to bed. Mrs. Cairns was old at the time, close to eighty and ailing, bedridden and in her final hours, but she was happy to make time to talk to me, one of Edgar's friends."

Silence descended on the room. All I could hear was the wind whistling around the corners of the brownstone buildings outside and a rhythmic banging faint in the lower levels of the building.

"I took her hand and asked her about Virginia and the

girl's parents. Virginia was the daughter of Maria, I wanted to know more about her. Mrs. Cairns was fading as we spoke, her blood pressure was falling and the white pallor of death was stealing across her face but she remained lucid, she shook her head and answered me, 'Oh no dear, Virginia wasn't Maria's. The poor girl was found, dear, a mile yonder on the stone steps of the city hall. Brought to me in a box as a bairn she was, blue and dying but I nursed her back to health and we brought her up us one of our own. It was easiest to simply pass her off as Maria's daughter to neighbors and such. When dear Edgar asked for her hand it seemed to clear everything up…and those two were so in love…" Her voice faded and her hand slowly slipped out of my own. I asked her quickly if she had told Edgar the truth of the matter and before she passed into unconsciousness she said faintly, 'never saw the point dear, they were so in love.' And then she was gone."

"And you never told Edgar?" Leah gasped.

"I could not at the time see how the news would help. Rather than marrying a first cousin, he had married a bastard infant raised to be his first cousin, how would that have been better received by the press and polite society? I decided to bury the conversation, at the time it wouldn't help the matter and could only make things worse."

The ladies considered and finally nodded agreement. To my surprise William had remained silent throughout the debate. He had ceased his endless looking out of the window and contemplation of his hands and was instead sat upright listening.

"William, are you ok? Do you hear something?"

He shook himself out of whatever trance he had put himself in and stood up from the table.

"No, sorry Joseph. A mood took me. I need some air."

He made his way suddenly to the door and opened it stepped into the space outside. He wound his way through the maze of mirrors and stopped in front of the large windows, a silhouette against the raging cloud and lashing rain beyond.

"So, if what we hear is correct, Edgar believed when he married Virginia, that he had found a way to cheat the devil, but unknowingly had condemned his wife to the exact fate he was certain he was avoiding."

I could sense that our time together was running short, my return to Baltimore was long overdue if I was to see Edgar alive once more.

"Ladies, if you would, how did you leave it with Edgar?"

Leah looked reluctant to continue the story, my mind tingled with the unspoken words the sisters casually shared between them.

"As kindly as we could we told Edgar all that we had discovered."

She paused, remembering the night, ten days ago, her face torn and full of sadness.

"The poor man was beyond himself, distraught. For many years he had deceived himself, the veil he wove was heavy and concealed the devil's contract even from himself. We offered what council we could, the exorcism of the beast was far beyond our powers, its claws deep within his soul. Freeing him from the beast would certainly break his mind."

"We provided him with our most precious talisman," continued Catherine, "an amulet made from pure silver and inscribed with the words of banishment 'Vade Retro Satana,' we wanted to make him stay with us, to keep him safe but he was in a rage, a mania had entered his mind and he wanted to leave the safety of our protection."

"Vade Retro Satana," I said translating the Latin, "Get behind me Satan."

"The words of Christ himself, during his temptation," said Margaretta, "the amulet is fabled to have been cast from a Tyrian shekel, one of the thirty pieces of silver used to buy the loyalty of Judas Iscariot and betray his lord to the Sanhedrin. It is a very precious and potent talisman, akin to the sword you carry. It would protect his spirit if not his mind. We counseled him to journey secretly and incognito. A disguise we provided to him, he would have appeared to any stranger as one of the thousands of ragged prospectors, heading for the Siskiyou trail and the promise of Californian gold. So attired he left us."

I nodded my head sadly in affirmation. So Edgar had fled into the night, left the safety of the Fox sister's and somehow returned several days later to Baltimore in the clothes they had provided to conceal his identity, the badly fitting black alpaca pantaloons, worn-out muddy boots and the tattered and palm leaf straw hat. The only missing piece was the amulet, it had not been found on his person. I pondered the puzzle in silence, wondering where such a precious thing could have disappeared when there was a commotion beyond the sliding wooden doors that separated the warehouse space from the stairs and corridor beyond. Someone was banging on the door. I stood and motioned the sisters to remain, and stepped into the lofty space looking for William who had disappeared from his spot by the windows. The banging was steady but insistent for more than a minute when it suddenly ceased. I walked slowly toward the door and was perhaps fifteen feet away when an explosion lifted me from my feet and deposited me on my back, ears deaf save a constant ringing, a cloud of brick dust heavy in the air. The detonation had splintered the large sliding warehouse doors, they hung in fragments and shards of timber, an open maul of sharp teeth. The mirrors closest to the door had either been destroyed by the blast or fallen, creating a wall of glass shards and timber. William was still nowhere to be seen and at the splintered door, as the ringing in my ears gradually abated, gruff voices could be heard in the corridor outside, voices filled with hate, The Dux de Obscurum, waiting for the smoke to clear so they could enter and wreak their havoc.

# *Chapter XXI*

*But the Raven, sitting lonely on the placid bust, spoke only*
*That one word, as if his soul in that one word he did outpour.*

The setting sun struggled to cast a final greasy light through the heavy windblown clouds outside his grimy window, as Ephraim Makepeace readied himself for work. He washed as best as he was able, swilling his armpits with the cold water from the dented and stained copper bowl he found a year ago, discarded in the alley beside the tavern he passed every night on his way home. He dragged his cleanest rough hemp shirt over his head and looked again at the gold coins he had taken from his keepsake tin. It had been four nights since his encounter with the stranger at the bar and there had been no contact from he or anybody else, no odd requests to allow access to the hospital or to see Edgar. Ephraim was beginning to think that luck may have, for once, glanced and smiled in his direction, the contract cancelled, the stranger gone, dead even, and he left with actual gold. The thought brought a crooked smile to his face and he let his thoughts run free for a moment, to what he could do with such money, clean clothes, a real mattress…a gas light for his house even! The thought made him giddy and he laughed out loud before placing the coins back inside the tin, replaced the painted lid and pushed it into the shadows far beneath his cot. Ephraim pulled on his ragged coat, too thin for the season, wrapped his scarf tight up around his ears and started to leave. A sudden thought came unbidden to his mind and he turned back and knelt again beside his cot, pulled the tin box out, slipped the amulet from its hiding place, leaving the coins behind, and deposited it mindlessly into his pocket. He pushed the box back into its hiding place and left, carefully locking the door behind him.

The wind was howling, an icy blast from the Patapsco river bowled him along Water Street in the direction of the hospital. The streets were quiet at that hour, dusk had settled across the city sent the good citizens to the safety of their homes. The gas lighters were patrolling the streets leaving pools of illumination across the walkways, banishing shadows in their path as they made their way along the sidewalks. Ephraim liked it better before the artificial lighting. He was a man more comfortable with darkness and secret places, shade and obscurity. Still, a light in his house, that would be nice, he could even pay a tutor to teach him his letters when he wasn't working, then he could read the book Moran had given him, improve himself, be able to help with more procedures. A promotion perhaps, and an increase in his wages. For once on his long cold walk he was happy, lost in his reverie and dreams, whistling tunelessly a contented melody of better times to come.

Something in the sky caught his eye and he looked up. The clouds were racing against the sky that had slowly turned to night. A large black sack had caught a gust of wind from some trash tossed carelessly into the alley between Old Man Shipham's Grocery store and the Tobacconists. He watched as it was turned and twisted, tossed carelessly by the gusts. It flew high and he almost lost sight of it against the black clouds, but at its apogee it stalled and turned back toward earth. It raced on the same sudden blast of frigid air that blew into his face and headed in his direction. He was enthralled and then horrified as the flying blackness took shape. The wind shifted, a strong gust against his back, but what he thought has been trash was now flying hard against the wind. Large black wings unfurled, a hooked beak above the glaring yellow eyes of a predator. The raven swooped down and Ephraim raised his arms in his defense. He ran for cover but the giant bird pursued him across the street, rising and striking, beating its black iridescent wings against his face and reaching with the claw of its beak for his eyes.

In his panic he saw an alley to his right and with a hand

in the air to keep the bird at bay he sprinted into the darkness. The gas lights on the street had narrowed his pupils and the alley was night cloaked, the darkness complete. He ran hard against an unmovable mass, banging and bloodying his nose. He felt a blade, jagged and razor sharp mark a line across his Adam's apple, held in place by a strong hand. His pupils finally permitted some light and he could discern three outlines. There were two short but burly shapes on either side and the tall man in front of him.

"I hope you have spent your coins well Ephraim Makepeace," said the tall man, and Ephraim's blood ran cold, his simple dreams trampled, discarded, yesterday's garbage. The contract remained in place, he was still bound by the ambiguous terms it imposed. A desperate thought sprang to his mind.

"I still have the gold, please let me return to my house, I will get them and gladly I will return them?"

The tall man laughed a low menacing chuckle, entirely bereft of humor.

"Oh no Ephraim, the coins cannot be returned, they are special you see, they can only be given by me, and only once in a lifetime. The time is now and the life is yours. I gave them to you in exchange for a service, a service not to be denied. Once given however, they become simple gold, please, spend them as you will, some soap perhaps or a change of clothing."

The men at his shoulders chuckled at the joke and Ephraim sighed, his shoulders slumped in resignation, so he was lost. His voice tired and defeated replied.

"What is it that you want from me?"

"But a trifle my friend. The client we represent is very concerned about the quality of treatment Edgar is receiving. We have a private hospital room and one of the best doctors at our disposable. In twenty-four hours' time we intend to move Edgar from the Washington College hospital to our facility."

"He is no prisoner, why not simply check him out tomorrow morning and move him then?" asked Ephraim.

"My client is generous to a fault, a great benefactor and prefers to remain anonymous. The deed must be done with an element of…stealth and secrecy." The tall man leant in, close to his face and the ebony eyes once more reflected his own gray, fear filled gaze. "Why else would we have employed your slithering skin Makepeace, would you deny me?" The question punctuated by a tightening arm and the blade creased deeper across his throat, a sliver of warm blood crept down his neck to stain his scarf.

Makepeace gasped, a mute note, unable to speak for fearing his Adam's apple would bob and cut itself against the blade, he shook his head…no…slowly, carefully and the pressure on the blade was eased.

"What would you have me do?"

"As I say a trifling matter," the tall man removed a large syringe from his pocket, wrapped it into a cotton bundle and slipped it into Makepeace's coat, "take this to Edgar's room tomorrow night and inject the sedative. Make sure you are not seen. Once you have administered it, go immediately to the college wing. You know the door they use to bring in cadavers for the medical students?"

"I do."

"Unlock it, walk away and return at once to your duties. Pay no more attention to the second floor and the private rooms, no matter what you hear or see, understood?"

Ephraim was shocked, silenced, his mind reeled with the consequences of such a deed but at the same time overwhelmed with the anticipation of the violence that would be summoned as reprisal if he refused to comply.

The tall man stepped closer and Ephraim could smell his breath and for the first time see his teeth. The breath was fetid flesh, the teeth small but black and each one filed to a point inside the cadaverous chasm of the mouth, "do you understand me Ephraim?" The words spoken slowly, each one emphasized, each one the cementing of a threat that would be faithfully executed. Ephraim had to turn away from the reek but nodded slowly, his voice lost, as he suspected, was his soul.

The tall man stepped back into the shadows and the knife was released from his throat, he was alone in the alley. He coughed and wiped the trickle of blood onto his scarf, his thoughts raced. He patted his pocket, hoped it was empty, but the long glass cylinder and steel plunger were there, the shape shrouded by the cotton but the outline undeniable, nestled closely against the amulet and its silver chain. Alone in the alley, dark dismay fell across his eyes.

# *Chapter XXII*

*Nothing farther then he uttered—not a feather then he fluttered—*
*Till I scarcely more than muttered "Other friends have flown before...*

The noise in the corridor subsided but the dust swirled in the chilly draught that entered the room from the broken door. The cloud of dust so thick even the door and the far wall were obscured. The faint outline of seven figures could be seen slowly emerging through the debris, four furtive outlines that spread out tactically and broadly across the room, the remaining three moved forward towards me. The man in the center was short but all of his cohorts were tall and broad. The two men behind the short man held something between them, slumped and heavy, they dragged it forward with them as they shortened the gap between us. I scrambled inelegantly to my feet, wiped a thin trickle of blood from my forehead, the remnant of a wood splinter that grazed me as I fell. The sisters were nowhere to be seen and I hoped that they had either escaped, or managed to conceal themselves in the room behind me. Outside, the evening was darkening, the rain lashing torrents across the broad windows blurred the city's buildings that were scattered across its skyline, an indistinct mountain range that reached across the fading horizon. The short leader walked forwards a few steps, and stopped to push some piles of broken timbers out of his way with a booted foot. In his hands was a wicked looking black iron knife, serrated and ugly and a long staff, topped by an orb that reflected darkly. My memory raced for a connection, I knew his stride and the way he held himself, the face was vague but familiar.

He grinned, showing me his small teeth, pointed behind thin dark lips.

"Don't you remember me Doctor Snodgrass," he rasped, "I am offended, but of course your type seldom recalls the names or faces of those who serve you. You may recall me as Kilmartin, Carter's butler, though that is neither my real name nor occupation as you can imagine."

"What do you want here?" I managed to say but my voice quavered, still in shock from the force of the detonation. My ears were still ringing and my balance was uncertain. I shook my head to clear the fog but it made me take a shaky step backwards to save myself from a fall. The man I knew as Kilmartin smiled at my awkwardness and obvious instability.

"We have come for the sisters Doctor, the sisters and the talisman that you brought here. You did well to bring them together for us. Two things much wanted and both difficult in their different ways to find. We must remember to thank you when our business here is concluded." His voice was a sneer across my mind, a snake's venomous coils that dripped with ill intent.

Kilmartin and his two burdened henchmen had continued to slowly draw forward, they stopped only ten feet from me. The other four had continued to spread out across the room, two to my right and two to my left. The dust was still settling, visibility was limited but I finally recognized the shape that slouched between the two intimidating figures that stood behind Kilmartin. The blond hair that fell across his face made him immediately recognizable.

"William," I gasped.

"The sisters if you would be so kind Snodgrass!"

There was no need to answer as a clicking of heels could be heard from the far end of the loft space. The sisters had appeared, side by side they slowly approached. At first glance they looked the same, dressed in black taffeta, raven black hair falling over their shoulders; the same and yet subtly different. As they walked, dance like in their fluid movements, colors fell across their dresses and lit the floor under their feet, blues, reds and purples splashed in sparks and glinted from the mirrors that lit their way. Their eyes showed no white sclera, only ebony black pupils filled their lids that flashed a hidden menace and threat. Kilmartin's eyes lit in anticipation and excitement, his prizes in sight. I used the distraction to move my hand to my pocket and curled my fingers around the grip of the Derringer. The sisters, far from hiding in the back room or making their escape had brought the fight to Kilmartin and I was eager to help if I could.

The sisters didn't hesitate or falter in their intent, they quickened their pace, moved in unison, dresses flowed, their heels threw multi-colored sparks that bounced off the mirrors that marked their passing. Suddenly they paused directly between the two huge black and carved frames of the antique mirrors that faced each other. The images of the sisters were instantly propagated through the reflections. Their individual powers were scaled and multiplied by the visceral connection to the unnatural realm they entered and summoned. The air thrummed with nascent power and the surfaces of the mirrors rippled and distorted with the stress of the containment. With a synchronized step, the sisters stamped the floor, a thunderclap aimed at Kilmartin. A broad but focused concussion of power was released and swept across the room in Kilmartin's direction, a conflagration of effort and will that consumed the very air it touched. The two henchmen behind Kilmartin cringed in anticipation just as the detonation swept them from their feet. Kilmartin didn't move, just leant into the storm that wrapped around him, burnt his features, melted the skin around his nose and mouth, blurred his features to a grimace. With the blast finally depleted, he smiled back at the sisters from the ruin of his mouth. I turned back to marvel at the women's fierce magic and concern swept through me. Their concerted effort had been costly to them, they looked fatigued, they breathed heavily, faces pale as they fought to recover.

Meanwhile the two brutes regained their feet still holding William between them. At Kilmartin's command they stretched his arms wide and Kilmartin took a step and swept his dark blade across William's chest. A wide streak of crimson flowed thickly from the cut and without hesitation Kilmartin plunged the orb of his staff into the flow of blood. At once the orb burst into a crackling flame that flickered with black and murky crimson intensity. He turned back to face the sisters and threw a ball of energy, pure puissance and loathing in their direction. The women still looked weary but they made themselves ready and as the pulsing sphere of energy reached them they stamped, danced a step back and pushed with all the strength of their beings against the abhorrence that threatened to consume them. The dark power, strengthened by the ritual act of desecration and sacrifice seemed too much for them to turn back against their attacker, but the women were discerning in their limitations and rather than directly challenge and block the power, they deflected, sideslipped, and with all of their combined powers they redirected the energy towards their mirrors.

The mirrors consumed the flickering ball of dark crimson across their many facets, held and refocused the energy it contained, a thousand reflections, an infinity of echoed images. The glass strained against the malevolence it was forced to consume, cracking and ringing harmonics built to a ringing crescendo until all of the smaller mirrors fractured as one, sent ten thousand daggers of glass flying back across the room towards the attackers. The two henchmen reflexively dropped William and covered their faces but the shards ripped through them, stabbed limbs and punctured organs, they fell, dead before they hit the floor. Kilmartin once more stood his ground, weathered the hail of splintered glass, his face torn from his skull, his clothes rent from his body. Finally, as the last shards fell to the floor at his feet, it stood, an amorphous shape, yellow flesh indistinct but whole, a creature revealed, inhuman. Its face was almost without features, no ears could be discerned, sunken pits where eyes should have been, its mouth was a black hole lined with small but sharpened teeth. Its body had been stripped bare by the assault, the skin was mottled yellow, taut across muscles that writhed beneath as it moved menacingly toward the sisters. It shouted to the four remaining thugs who were still spread out across the space.

"Attack! Seize the whores!" Its voice harsh from the maul of the hole in its face.

The women had suffered from the concerted effort to repel the dark energy; Leah's shoulder looked to be dislocated, she held her right arm awkwardly across her chest, face drained of color she looked about to swoon. Catherine and Margaretta had kept their feet, dark hair plastered across ashen brows but their eyes retained a ferocity I had never thought to witness. They faced the creature together as it approached.

To my shock, but extreme relief I saw William slowly and painfully crawling away towards the windows, a trail of sticky blood painted his trail. The four thugs had begun to convene, walked quickly towards the injured women. I pulled the Derringer from my pocket and aimed at the back of the creature's head, certain that such an earthly weapon could cause the monster no harm but resolute in my attempt to try anyway, when a large bulky shape appeared through the brick dust and debris of the shattered door, moving quickly but silently, running, leaping over the ruin of broken timber. His footsteps barely made a sound, he rapidly closed the ground on the four thugs. He slammed into the man on the far left sending him to the floor. In a single fluid motion the welcome stranger rolled over his victim's body, his arm coiled around the thug's neck as he turned, breaking it in one seamless move, the noise clear and sickly across the now silent room. The other thug took a step backwards in shock and surprise but was already recovering and reaching into his jacket for a weapon. The stranger half rose, one hand on the floor, knees bent and I saw his face below the brim of the brown derby he wore, pale colorless eyes in a broad Slavic face. Darko had come to our aid, unexpected but hugely welcomed. He motioned at me, towards the thug who was still trying to release his pistol, and pushed off on his right foot and passed me, quickly closing the distance on his next targets, the two men to my right. I pulled the Derringer from my pocket, cocked the trigger and fired a shot at the thug who had finally managed to free and raise his pistol. I aimed for the center of his chest, hoping for a kill shot to the heart or a ruptured lung but the heavy slug from the unfamiliar weapon flew high and caught him left of center of his chin, shattered his jaw. Teeth and blood flew into the air as he sank to the ground.

Darko raced across the space and closed on the two men to the right of me, leapt into the air and landed with a devastating drop kick on one man that must have broken ribs. The second henchman tried to center his pistol on Darko but Darko was agile and unnervingly fast, after landing his kick he was already pivoting and ducking under the man's aim. The pistol fired, a deafening crack in the echoing space but the bullet flew harmlessly away. Darko performed a fluid forward roll to land at the man's feet and rose quickly bringing the top of his head sharply under the assailant's chin. There was a grunt from the man and his knees buckled, Darko pivoted inside the man's space taking the arm holding the pistol over his right twisting shoulder. Darko bent his knees  and threw the thug high over his shoulder to land hard and broken at his feet.

Darko looked once more in my direction, his visage flat and emotionless, balanced easily on the balls of his feet, hands relaxed at his side, he was the epitome of readiness and surety. We both turned to face the creature, Leah had stumbled backwards and leant awkwardly on the frame of a mirror to her side, her body shaking and face ashen. The creature held the black jagged blade and staff, a hazard toward Catherine and Margaretta who held their ground as it stalked across the small space that separated them. The women looked small, as the creature, released from Kilmartin's body rose to its full height and loomed toward them; their eyes were downcast and they appeared defeated as the orb was raised to crash down on Catherine's forehead, the black iron blade poised to strike at Margaretta's eyes. As the weapons descended on their killing trajectories, the women raised their eyes in an ebony blaze and simultaneously took each other's hands. Arms stretched out from their sides they reached a hand toward and through the glass of the mirrors that still stood on either side of them, making contact with the unknowable powers that lurked across the dark divide. The creature was instantly enveloped in a silver luminescence that paralyzed it. The stress on Catherine and Margaretta was palpable, they visibly shook with the effort but Darko was already moving to offer what assistance he could. He was only a man, mere flesh and blood against the pure maleficence of the creature and I doubted even his effectiveness, but still he closed the gap intent on his prey. The creature emitted a ghastly scream of frustration and writhed against the strength of its captors, forced a silent scream from the women as they struggled to restrain it. I had one shot left and raised the barrel of my pistol and took sight, finger hard against the trigger, but before I could shoot, the blade of the talisman sword, crimson with the creature's dark blood, jutted suddenly and brutally out of its chest. The blade burned, iridescence rippled across its edges, illuminated the delicate etchings, set flame to each sigil as the beast looked down in shock and disbelief. Catherine and Margaretta sagged with relief and withdrew their hands from beyond the mirrors shining surface. The sword became a blaze, a coruscation of white light that burnt the creature from within even as the blade itself melted away. The demon trembled and writhed horribly, until, with its life force spent, it released the iron knife and staff from its clutches. The iron rang on the floor and the orb shattered on impact, sent a shimmer of black energy across the floor that scorched all that it touched. Finally, the creature slid wetly to the floor. William was stood in its place, between the trembling sisters, hands still cupped where the swords hilt had been, a look of hatred and vengeance dark across his fair features.

# *Chapter XXIII*

*On the morrow he will leave me, as my Hopes have flown before."*
*Then the bird said "Nevermore."*

Tendrils of smoke began to rise from the body of the creature and we all took a step backwards as the smell, rank and fetid, rose from the corpse and assailed our nostrils. William fell to his knees, the front of his shirt crimson from the blood he had lost. Leah finally succumbed to unconsciousness, her knees buckled and she would have fallen heavily had Darko not been prescient enough to anticipate and step quickly to catch her. She lay in his arms, a pile of limbs, a sweep of ebony hair obscured her face. He carried her, twenty feet to a space in front of the windows and lowered her gently to the floor, a safe space, not covered in broken glass, and sufficiently far from the stench of the monster's carcass that continued to steam and smoke.

Holding my breath I stepped across the smoking body to take hold of William's shoulders and half carried, half dragged him to where Leah now lay. Margaretta and Catherine walked unsteadily across to join us and with the exception of Darko we all sank to the floor to share a stunned but thankful silence. I knew my help was needed, perhaps urgently in William's case, but we all needed a few minutes to regain our normal selves. I stared out beyond our reflections, out across the city skyline, searched the horizon for an early sign of dawn, the harbinger of a new day and renewed hope, but the windows looked out west across the black ribbon of the river below us and permitted me no such view.

Darko had been busy and brought water and blankets, bandages and some ointments he had found in the office and the bathrooms that lay behind. He shook me, not too gently by the shoulder and looked across at William and Leah who lay wounded. In his heavy accent he demanded.

"You are needed here Doctor…now."

I sighed and with a groan heaved myself to my feet and went about my work. Leah was still unconscious so with Darko's help we sat her upright and took the opportunity to relocate her dislocated shoulder. I bent the arm to ninety degrees at the elbow and slowly rotated until I felt resistance. With a quick look at Darko who nodded and held her head and tightly secured her uninjured arm, I quickly raised and rotated the arm in the sagittal plane and with a startlingly loud click slipped the humeral back into the glenoid fossa. Darko nodded again, this time with an acknowledgment toward my proficiency. He covered her with one of the blankets and we moved across to William. He lay conscious, blue eyes open but deathly still, his right arm across the line of his wound. I peeled his arm carefully away, which made his face pucker in a grimace. He let out a low groan as I cut the remains of his shirt open, my heart in my mouth expecting the cut to have entered his abdominal cavity, severing the intestines or puncturing the liver. I probed the wound carefully, and was enormously relieved to find that the muscles of the abdominal wall were intact. The cut was deep and had severed several small blood vessels. The blood loss was visually disturbing but practically minimal. Apart from being extremely sore for several days, he merely required fluids and pain killers. I smeared a tincture of carbolic acid across the wound and bound him tight with the surgical gauze Darko had discovered. Darko tipped a bottle of water to his lips and William gulped gratefully. William wiped his chin and his face, and thankfully returned my smile with a weak one of his own. I finally checked on Margaretta and Catherine who were both exhausted but unhurt. Margaretta had retrieved the creatures evil looking iron blade that only minutes before had threatened to skewer her, turned it over and over in her hands, examined the strange design with open curiosity. Darko had disappeared, slipped away on some errand of his own.

Darko had been relentless in his efforts, in the office he had prepared food, some kind of hot stew and brewed coffee for everybody. Leah had started to come around and our small group limped and shuffled to sit more comfortably in the cozy room. Darko appeared at my side and whispered.

"I need to dispose of the creature's cadaver, it stinks and its flesh burns the floor. The bodies of its followers also need to be removed and the room made secure once more."

I nodded approval and he slipped soundlessly away.

The stew was hot and the meat was flavored with sweet paprika and garlic, it burnt my lips and gave energy and comfort in equal measures. The coffee was so rich and strong it made my head hurt and I gulped it down, drained my mug and poured myself another. We could hear Darko outside but left him to his labor, not one of us had either the energy or will to help him deal with the pile of corpses. The color had returned to Leah's face and she didn't even seem to be aware that her shoulder had suffered a dislocation. She looked across at me.

"It pains me to say it Joseph, William, but very soon we all need to leave this place. It has remained secret and hidden for decades, but now its location is known, we are certain to be attacked again. And next time they will not fail, they will send a legion."

I nodded slowly as I finished the last spoonful of stew, setting the spoon down heavily in the bowl.

"We are ready to leave Leah. I can only apologize for the havoc we have unintentionally brought down upon your home. We could not stay even if we wished it be so, we are needed back in Baltimore, if Edgar has not already died, I sense that Carter, who went there to provide protection, will need all the help he can muster."

I looked across at the three sisters, sat now quietly together, plain ordinary black taffeta dresses, gentle in demeanor, dust in their hair and scratches across their tired faces. The discolored and tarnished mirror on the wall behind them reflected the disheveled raven hair that fell down their backs.

"And you, ladies, where will you journey to. Will you come with us, would you lend us your aid?"

"No Joseph, we will fight to protect our home but this is not our war. We will move to another place, a veiled and…" Leah struggled with the correct word to describe what she wanted to say, finally, "obscure location. Our time in New York, in the lives of men and women of this world is over. Complete. We are lessened and so will join the hermetic order, secrete ourselves away and move beyond this plane of existence."

I could only guess at what she meant but it seemed clear that we would not be able to rely on the formidable aid they could have brought and I suspected this would be our last meeting. Darko returned to stand in the doorway, he was panting with his exertions but his face was impassive as always and he stood balanced and ready to accept any challenge.

"We must leave soon, Doctor Snodgrass, Captain Walker, a train leaves for Baltimore this very night and we are needed there most urgently. We will be safe here for a few short hours and should rest, but soon we need to go."

I nodded agreement, the dread and horror of the last few hours had turned into a vast lake of fatigue that I could feel myself falling towards. William was the same, his head was nodding already, his breathing heavy. I turned to face the sisters.

"One last question," I said, "what is…what was, Kilmartin. What sort of beast was he?"

I expected Leah to answer but instead she deferred to Darko, a strange look in her eyes, a guilty tilt to her head as she looked through the curtain of dark hair that had fallen down her face. I looked back at Darko, still resting in the doorway, William turned in his chair, eliciting a grunt of discomfort as he twisted.

His mien was as always stoical, inscrutable and dispassionate but he looked back at Leah and I could sense the tension between them. Finally, reluctantly he spoke.

"The creature was not Kilmartin. The real Kilmartin was indeed Doctor Carter's butler, a man made of flesh and blood who served us well for many years. We now know that he was captured by the Dux de Obscurum several nights ago. Captured and tortured for the information he retained and stripped of his skin. The creature wore his face and flesh like a second skin to deceive. In my country, the old world, such creatures are known as Furies, the daughters of Nyx, the Goddess of night. Her daughters are three in number, they are named Alecto, Megaera and Tisiphone. Three sisters, appearing in forms of their own choosing, wearing the flesh of others to conceal themselves, each one very potent and difficult to destroy. Only a mighty talisman like the sword or one of the sisters can end their lives. Captain Walker killed one tonight and the sword was destroyed, but I fear the other two will be ready to meet us when we return to Baltimore."

I looked back to shout an appeal for help from the women, but the room was empty of the sisters, they had gone, disappeared. I thought for a second I could see a glimpse of floating taffeta within the obscure reflection of the mirror but in a moment it too had disappeared from sight.

# *Chapter XXIV*

*Startled at the stillness broken by reply so aptly spoken,*
*"Doubtless," said I, "what it utters is its only stock and store*

After his confrontation with the raven and the tall man, Ephraim had completed his shift in a daze. With Moran himself hospitalized, a young junior doctor called Donovan had taken his place on the night shift. Donovan was barely twenty-two, he wore his chestnut hair too long but his dark brown eyes shone with enthusiasm and an eagerness to learn. Moran himself had taken him under his wing, occasionally helping him with his studies. He was in his fourth year and would have started the night shift straight after a nine hour shift on the wards below. The young man was keen but like many starting in his profession he was overworked, stressed and exhausted and each night Makepeace had found him in the attendee's office, his body deep in the leather chesterfield, feet propped on the leather topped oak desk, and a medical journal opened and draped over his eyes, sleeping deeply. It meant that the normal duties of the night shift fell on Makepeace himself and luckily there were now only two occupants in the private rooms, Edgar and Moran.

He had already checked on Moran who had been sleeping soundly in his bed. Moran turned over, perhaps sensed his presence in the room, but he didn't wake. The door to his locker was open so he pushed it silently closed with his foot and went next door to check on Edgar Allan Poe. The poor man had not recovered, in fact his condition was worsening. He was thin and ashen faced, still murmuring nonsense words in his sleep. Ephraim stared at the face for a long time, trying to understand what the tall man and his cohorts could want with one so wretched. Regardless, it seemed a shame that even in his last days he was soon to be abducted and subjected to god alone knew what. He sighed deeply and touched the syringe still wrapped in his pocket, the syringe he would use in less that twenty-four hours to enable the man's abduction.

He walked home after his shift, despondent and afraid. Afraid of the course of action he had been coerced into, afraid for the life of the victim the tall man pursued, afraid for his own life and above all, mortally afraid for his own soul. Every noise made him jump, every movement around a dark corner or down some unwholesome alleyway made him start. He knew he was being watched though he saw nobody.

The day had passed as if in a trance. He had slept fitfully and woken in the afternoon to make some thin soup from some old vegetable scraps the cook at the hospital had spared him. He opened the keepsake box under his bed and removed the two gold coins. They felt hot in his hands and he took the amulet from his pocket to compare them. The amulet was cool bright silver, still gleaming in the dirty light that spilled weakly through his grimy windows. The blood red gold of the coins made his hands sweat. In his left palm, the coins. In his right the amulet. The gold was heavy, dense and precious; the amulet was light in his hands and yet possessed a depth to its glimmer, a purity of form and beauty that far surpassed the intrinsic value of the coins. Finally, he placed the coins back in their box and threw the open box onto his dirty cot. It no longer seemed to matter to him if the coins were stolen. He had become a dead man walking. His quiet life in his beloved hovel seemed to be on the edge of a precipice, one to which he was running towards. Without thinking, he pocketed the amulet, absent mindedly making sure it was deep in his pocket and perfectly safe.

# *Chapter XXV*

*Caught from some unhappy master whom unmerciful Disaster*
*Followed fast and followed faster till his songs one burden bore…*

Darko woke me in a room still submerged in complete darkness. He shook my shoulder surprisingly gently and whispered.

"Doctor Snodgrass, it is time…"

I stretched a little and tried to shake off the stupor of too little sleep. The fatigue still stretched across my bones, but I sensed deeply that time was racing away from us and we still had far to go. After waking me, Darko had left to light a candle in the large space beyond the door and I could see his shadow moving, packing and preparing for our departure.

The few blankets that Darko had found had provided a bed of sorts and the overwhelming fatigue both William and I had felt the night before had aided our sleep. William was waking and looked something close to himself again, he groaned as he stretched and he swept the hair from across his eyes, self-consciously hiding his scar, as he sensed me looking across at him. I thought back to the night we had met at Martick's only five nights prior and his willingness to join me on this venture. I wondered darkly if he was regretting that decision. He had barely escaped with his life, wounded by the creature and then forced to fight and take its life with the sword. I started to rise, stiffly and awkwardly, uncoiling my lanky limbs from my position on the floor when the door opened and Darko stepped inside. He looked no different, neither tired nor refreshed. I suspected he had been outside all night, sleeplessly guarding the broken door.

There had been no further sign of the sisters, wherever they had disappeared to, whatever curious realm they now inhabited, it seemed that there they would remain. The succor they could offer in our desperate need, withdrawn.

"We must leave Doctor, our train leaves in a little over an hour," said Darko.

I sighed but nodded thanks and walked over to where William still lay on the floor. I offered a hand and he took it, stepped clumsily to his feet but with only the slightest help from me. I quickly checked his wound which was livid red but healing well and we stepped together back into the vast room where only yesterday we had first met the sisters. The two antique mirrors closest to us still stood unbroken, facing each other, reflected the few amber gas lights on the city streets. The Hudson swept by below us, glittering in the scarce moonlight that broke through the clouds. I walked over to the two mirrors and stood once more between them. I saw myself darkly reflected a hundred times, disappearing into the infinity of reflections, but without Leah's influence there was only myself. No dark shadow stood behind me as far back as I could see, and I wondered gravely if that was a good or a bad omen.

Darko's reflection appeared in the mirror behind me and interrupted my melancholy. I turned to take a moment to survey the ruin of the room. He had disposed of the bodies, I didn't want to consider where or how, but I suspected the Hudson had played a dark role. There remained a large spread of fractured glass, shards and sharp fragments scattered across the floor. Blood spatters lay strewn amidst the slivers of glass, congealed and drying to a viscous brown. I shuddered at the memory of the violence and remembered Darko's role in our redemption. His unexpected appearance had saved all of our lives. I turned to face him and looked into his ghostly pale eyes.

"How did you know you would be needed here, and how did you follow us without being seen?"

"I didn't know I would be needed. Doctor Carter demanded that I should follow you. As for not being seen," the slightest shade of a smile appeared on his normally impassive face, "that was easy, you and the young Captain seem to be oblivious to peril. The beast that was

Kilmartin, and his cohorts, followed you onto the train in Richmond. I simply had to follow them. That is where I almost failed in my duty," he looked at me directly in the eyes and tilted his head in apology, "you and William Walker managed to get to Manhattan on the same ferry as Kilmartin's gang, the ferry you caught left before I myself could get to the dockside. By the time I arrived at the Fox sister's residence, I heard the explosion that destroyed the doors and granted them entrance. The rest you know."

"I owe you my life, as does William and the Fox sisters, you far from failed in your duty Mr. Darko. Please call me Joseph." I held out my hand and he reached across and covered it in his giant gnarled paw. I nodded my head and he nodded his in turn and we shook once, a seal of a forgiveness for our treatment in Richmond and a nod towards our strange but welcome friendship. His gaze returned to its natural state of bland inscrutability and he turned and stepped across the rubble of the splintered door. William approached from behind, gave me a curious wink having witnessed the interaction with our rescuer, and with a final look back across the sister's former hiding place we turned our backs on it and followed Darko's passage back down the stairs and into the cold wind that howled up Stone Street from the direction of the Hudson to our right.

We arrived at Liberty Pier early and had to wait, frustrated and chilled, looking across to the skyline of Jersey. The elongated glass canopied dome of Paulus Hook station could just be discerned in the gloom of the pre-dawn. Lying close the water, the prow of the steam ferry New Brunswick cut a silver wake across the deep purple of the river, dark under the heavy stratocumulus that streamed overhead. The steamer approached and with a hard turn of her rudder and a high spray of water from her sunken paddles she rolled broadside to the pier and was quickly secured by coils of hawsers that stood ready, speedily deployed by many hands who appeared from nowhere to ready the ship for a quick turnaround. We were quickly onboard and enjoyed the solitude and safety of the crossing. Gulls were raucous in the sky and the saltwater splashed our faces. For a few moments we were safe, isolated and beyond the reach of the world of demons and evil creatures that had slipped unbidden into our own. Too quickly the crossing was completed and we headed toward the railway terminal.

For the first time I paid attention to the way Darko moved and I understood what he meant by his comment on the manner in which we blithely walked into danger. He walked a few yards away from us and the flow of other passengers, constantly scanning his field of view for threats, turning his head slightly to eradicate blind spots. Unrelentingly vigilant, attentive to every nook and cranny, every person who entered his sight was examined and evaluated. I endeavored to be more aware and watchful myself, who knew how long we would have the man's help, and it seemed that as we got closer to returning to Baltimore, the hazards and menace would only increase.

We boarded the train and William and I took our seats for the long, almost twelve hour trip back to our friend Edgar in Baltimore. Darko disappeared immediately, walked the length of the train's carriages to check for hidden enemies and concealed threats. At exactly four o'clock in the morning the train whistle blew and the carriage jolted forward against its couplings. Smoke filled the canopy of the station and we rattled slowly forwards to finally escape the confines of the concourse. The familiar yards, filled with carriages passed us by and then we were flying through the late fall countryside of New Jersey. The fields were still hidden and bleak, barren from the recent tobacco harvest, the snow from the journey north two nights ago had melted, leaving them black under the clouds.

Darko returned and sat heavily in the seat across from myself, his bulk forced William to shuffle across on the bench, closer to the window. It was clear we had both deferred to Darko's abilities in the venture as William turned and asked.

"What now Mr. Darko? What awaits us in Baltimore?"

He considered the question for a few minutes as he looked out across the country that flew in a blur past the window. He spoke quietly, his accented voice hard to follow across the noise of the swaying carriage.

"The Fury that Mr. Walker killed was named Megaera, the two remaining Furies, Alecto and Tisiphone will have sensed the loss of one of their kind. The creatures are ancient and have survived together for centuries. Such a loss will be a blow to them but they will now be vengeful and dangerous beyond comprehension. If they were apart for some reason it is certain that they will be doing everything they can to return to each other. I fear that in Baltimore we will find them reunited."

"You mentioned that the sisters had the power to defeat such a being?" William asked.

"Yes, but they have distanced themselves from this world. We are unlikely to see their kind again on this earth. Doctor Carter would know more, but to my knowledge only one other weapon exists with the same power as the talisman that William used to kill the creature."

"Another sword?" I asked.

"No, the sword was unique and its loss is costly to the world that remains. The other talisman, the only one with the power to destroy a Fury is in the form of an amulet, a simple silver circle hung on a simple silver chain."

# *Chapter XXVI*

*Till the dirges of his Hope that melancholy burden bore*
*Of 'Never—nevermore'."*

There had been no time to make reservations in the sleeper carriages, and by the time we had boarded and spoken to the conductor, they had all been taken, so we spread out on the bench seating in the first class cabin and made ourselves as comfortable as was possible. I nodded in my seat, forehead pressed hard against the window, my head vibrating in time with the thrust of the engine's piston. Every hard bounce of the locomotive's wheels across the rails woke me slightly and I slitted my eyes to see the night streaking by outside our window, a blur of fields, telegraph poles, and occasionally, a darkened cottage pressed hard up against the railway lines. William was fast asleep, squashed hard between the window and the bulk of Darko, who was of course, wide awake and watching, wary and vigilant of the small amount of foot traffic that padded up and down the carriage. My eyes closed and finally, exhausted, I slept.

I woke for a few minutes as the train paused its journey in Philadelphia. There was the usual hubbub of departing and arriving passengers, baggage stowed and seats being taken. I watched Darko watching the new arrivals, his pale gaze carefully guarded below the brim of the brown derby he refused to remove. The train slowly pulled out of the smoke darkened station and accelerated slowly through the suburbs of the city and crossed the Schuylkill River on the rusting iron Grays Ferry Railway Bridge. The morning sunshine shone weakly, diffused through low clouds that clustered behind empty fields, framed by the golden yellow and russets of the Northern Red Oaks and Black Spruce that marked our passing. The motion of the train called me back to sleep, and I managed to sprawl my limbs somewhat comfortably across the otherwise empty bench seat. The urgent passage of time shouted in frustration to me, but despite its racket and the rattle of the carriage I slipped once more towards slumber.

I woke to a cloud filled afternoon. The rain that streaked across the windows of the train made the countryside through which we passed bleary and indistinct. William was awake, staring out of the window. Darko was nowhere to be seen. William heard me yawn and looked across, a warm smile on his lips, a glean of excitement in his blue eyes. He pushed his spectacles back up to the bridge of his nose.

"We are approaching Baltimore. I ordered some coffee when I saw that you were waking."

"A thousand thanks," I said, my voice a rasp, "I must have slept for hours."

"Yes, but we sensed that you needed it, so we let you rest."

I stretched and gave out a low groan. I might have slept, but a bed would have done my poor joints better service.

"Where is Darko?"

"Hunting potential bounders and mountebanks I believe. The man never rests and suspects everybody."

I smiled an amused agreement, "yes, but he did save our lives."

William didn't respond, instead he turned to watch the countryside slowly populate with houses as we approached the outskirts of the city. I knew he didn't like Darko so changed the subject.

"How are you feeling now?"

"Tender still, but healing well thanks to you."

I waved his thanks away, "how far from Baltimore are we?"

"Only a few minutes I think, Green Mount Cemetery lies to our right."

I looked out of the window to where he indicated. Sure enough the familiar Gothic spire of the chapel and rows of white marble gravestones were visible through the rain steamed window and drizzle beyond.

"I feel we will be too late. We should have returned instead of Carter."

"Perhaps, but we make the decisions we do based on the alternative choices available. Not all paths can be seen and some…are simply not open to us. I stand by the decision I made that night, at Martick's, to join you on this trip. For myself, I am happy I came."

He reached a hand across and laid it on top of mine.

"True friendship in this world can be hard to find Joseph. I am glad to call you my mine."

I smiled a little sadly. I had few true friends in the world. Colleagues yes, but no real friendships. This adventure had made me less self-aware of my illness and the appearance it had imposed on me. It had given me confidence to stand straight and look the world a little straighter in the eye. I moved my other hand and placed it over William's.

"And I am pleased beyond measure to call you mine."

A smile cracked my face and I laughed out loud, eliciting some looks from the other occupants of the carriage who looked our way, some shaking heads, to see two grown men holding hands. The laugh felt good, a release of the stress, horror and pent up emotions of the last few days. William returned my laugh, and so Darko found us, his face betraying nothing he sat impassively by William's side, his expression a complete blank, which made us both laugh more, silly and carefree for just a moment.

Our moment of humor was interrupted by the porter who came by with the coffee. We broke hands and sat more properly in our seats as he poured three mugs, and taking his leave, he left the pot behind. The train whistle signaled our approach to Baltimore and the braking motion of the train jolted us forward, forcing William to pause in bringing the coffee to his lips.

"We must consider our actions when we arrive," said Darko.

"Do you have a plan?" I asked.

"If all has gone well with Doctor Carter, he and Volk will have united with Doctor Moran. From there they would have gone to rescue your friend Edgar Allan Poe."

"And if things have not gone as expected?"

He gave a shrug of his large shoulders and a stoic grunt. The train jolted once more, rounded a tight turn to the right and then braked hard as the Italianate inspired architecture of the new brick built Camden Street Station hove into sight.

"Then it will fall to us to rescue him," was his simple response.

# *Chapter XXVII*

*But the Raven still beguiling all my fancy into smiling,*
*Straight I wheeled a cushioned seat in front of bird, and bust and door;*
*Then, upon the velvet sinking, I betook myself to linking…*

The time had finally come, a full night and day had passed since the knife had bloodied his throat. He sat shivering on his bed, absentmindedly fingered the chain and amulet in his pocket, silently prayed to a god he didn't believe in, to redeem him from a sin he didn't want to commit. What he expected to be his last shift at the hospital began in less than an hour, so with a heave and a sigh he stood, shoulders bent, a look of defeat smeared across his features. The tin lay open on his cot, the gold coins had spilled from the box. The once precious metal, a window of opportunity to a better life tossed carelessly. He hated the feel of the gold, eschewed its touch.

His head ached with the stress, the same thoughts repeated, running around his mind. How had he come to this point? Was there a way out he had not considered? The questions cycled without answer and he let out one last sigh, retrieved the small red leather bound treatise that Moran had kindly lent him and finally left his small house. He walked out into the dusk without closing his door or pausing to take one last look at the life he left behind.

The walk to the hospital was uneventful, no ravens pursued him, no dark strangers lurked dangerously in alleys. No other enemies but the torments of his own thoughts were needed, they pursued him relentlessly, tormented him without mercy. The wind screamed across the wet streets, rain hammered against his face but he felt nothing. His mind was divorced from the steps he took towards the hospital. His legs acted autonomously, closed the distance to his doom, footfall by footfall he stepped carelessly through puddles, drenched his worn shoes. The rain soaked him through making him tremble involuntarily.

He was still trembling when he opened his locker on the first floor staff room and exchanged his wet coat and bloodstained scarf for his slightly less than white hospital coat. He washed his hands in the steel sink and scrubbed to a lather with the carbolic soap provided for the use of the hospital's employees. He looked in the mirror, stared hard at the familiar face, one he thought he knew. The eyes looking back were changed, unfamiliar. He had always known that he was hard featured, ill-favored, but now he looked broken, the eyes bleak and unseeing, haunted by acts he knew he must carry out, but wished with his entire being that it were not so.

He took his time washing and scouring, his eyes locked to his own in the mirror. With hands clean he took the stiff nail brush and dug deep with the bristles below each grimy snagged nail. For once he took pleasure in the routine, tried to erase the memory of the encounter with the tall man, washed the touch of violence and the threat to his safety and sanity, watched the grime swirl down the drain and wished it were that easy to rinse his promises and liberate his soul.

# *Chapter XXVIII*

*Fancy unto fancy, thinking what this ominous bird of yore—*
*What this grim, ungainly, ghastly, gaunt, and ominous bird of yore*
*Meant in croaking "Nevermore."*

With his hands as clean as they had ever been, Makepeace walked slowly up the staircase to the second floor. The second floor wing of the hospital was empty except for the two patients and the attending physician, Doctor Donovan. Makepeace made his way down the corridor towards the office, carefully silenced each footstep, bided his time. His elongated shadow, thrown by the meagre light of the few lamps that were left to burn at this time of night, stalked alongside him, projected a ghoul onto the tiled walls. Outside the office he peered in and found Donovan fast asleep as expected, feet on the leather topped oak desk, and a journal opened and draped over his eyes, dead to the world. If left undisturbed he would sleep till dawn.

He set off back down the corridor toward the patient's rooms, fingered the syringe in his pocket and continued to weigh his limited options as he went. Edgar's room was halfway along the corridor, the door was open but the room inside was silent and dark. Makepeace took a candle and lit it from the gas sconce in the corridor and made his way across to the recumbent form of the sleeping patient. The man was still shackled to his bed. He seemed to be not long for this world and Makepeace wondered once more, what use this "client" of the tall man would have for one so close to death.

Edgar's eyes were tight shut, the bruising around his mouth had faded to the color of bruised peaches. The bandages were still tightly wrapped around his ears but at least tonight his respiration was slow and clear, tonight he slept in peace. Makepeace reached into his pocket and retrieved the syringe, unwrapped it from its cotton shroud.

He shook the glass cylinder and the brown liquid inside slid, a viscous ooze along the barrel. He shook his head in despair, rolled up the sleeve of the hospital gown, muttered a small prayer to himself, not really knowing the correct words, or if forgiveness was sought for the deed he was about to commit or for the absolution of his own soul.

"Lord forgive me," he whispered, his voice strained with misery and defeat.

He slowly exerted pressure on the syringe, the needle easily punctured Edgar's crepe parchment skin. His thumb was poised over the plunger, heart pounding, about to press and release the vials contents into Edgar's arm when a commotion in the next room made his heart skip a beat and he froze. He listened intently until he finally made out Moran's voice from the next room. Moran was in the midst of a nightmare, shouting and struggling in the room next door.

Makepeace was frozen into inaction. His slow mind churned the implications, tried to weigh the cost of his survival over that of this poor man in his hands and his friend in the next room. Another shout from Moran, almost a scream, made him jump, and the combined weight of the leather treatise and the pretty silver amulet in his pocket banged against his thigh. Clarity sprang to his mind and simple concern for Moran finally overwhelmed him. He carefully slipped the needle from Edgar's arm, and still holding the syringe rushed into the adjacent room to help Moran.

He found the doctor tangled in bedsheets, clawing the air in front of himself as if to defend his face from some attack. He grabbed the doctor and shook him gently, whispered words of comfort in an attempt to bring him out of the nightmare that was stressing his already damaged heart. Moran slowly calmed and finally lay back peacefully on the bed, shaken and breathing heavily but slowly waking from whatever night terror had stalked him. With his patient finally restored and relaxed he whispered.

"I will make you some tea Doctor, I know how you like your tea. It will revive you and calm your nerves. We need to keep you calm."

Makepeace lit the candle by the bed and then turned and left the room, slipped the syringe into the pocket of his gown as he turned to leave the room. Outside in the corridor he leant heavily against the wall, gasping for air and pondering what to do next. Returning to Edgar's room was clearly out of the question. With Moran awake and his own resolve shaken, he no longer had either the inclination or the opportunity to carry out the deed the tall man had demanded. He walked slowly back down the broad stairs to the ground floor.

As he stepped into the entrance vestibule, the vast open space consumed him and the enormity of his failure struck him. He staggered, almost to his knees and had to grab the cold stone handrail of the staircase to steady himself. He only had one desperate thought. He needed to check if the tall man was here waiting in the shadows outside the mortuary doors. Perhaps there was a chance to tackle him and maybe even defeat him, even use the syringe and its evil contents against him.

He made his way feebly along the ground floor corridor toward the teaching wing. The double folding doors pushed easily open. The vast room was empty, dark and devoid of life. He weaved his way through the room full of surgical trolleys and tables stacked high with steel instruments, bowls and cloths. During daylight this space would be filled with young junior doctors at work dismembering corpses, retrieving and dissecting organs, performing practice operations and then suturing the wounds on the cold uncaring flesh. There were large doors to the mortuary, a chilled space at the rear of the room where fresh cadavers were brought. Two large locked iron doors lay beyond, if the tall man was here he would be waiting outside them.

Breathing hard, his feet leaden, he tried to approach the

iron doors quietly. His hand reached out and carefully touched the cold iron surface. No vibration could be felt so he leaned in slowly, carefully, and pressed his ear up against the chill of the metal. No sound could be heard, outside the night was silent. He once more grabbed the syringe in his left hand, held it like a dagger, thumb hard against the flange of the plunger and with his right hand he reached out to the key in the heavy lock that protected him from the outside.

He started to turn the key, iron grated on iron, the springs squeaked on the tumblers as they turned and fell into place, one by one released their hold on the door. A faint scratching sound from beyond the doors made Makepeace stop, heart thumping. One tumbler secured him and his hospital from whatever lay beyond. He waited and listened, strained with all of his senses to determine if somebody waited outside in the dark of the night. Minutes passed but no further noise could be heard so with a final turn the last tumbler fell with a click that seemed to reverberate throughout the hospital. His hand fell away from the key and he raised the syringe shoulder high poised to stab the tall man or at least one of the brutes from the alley.

He pushed the door gently outward an inch or two and it swung slowly, a grating groan of unoiled iron against the rusting casement into the night beyond. Makepeace peered out, his right eye close to the gap. He tried to remain silent but he panted noisily and his breath plumed outward into the frigid night air.

At first he could determine nothing, the inky blackness of the night defeated his light constricted pupils that strained to adjust. Then a movement to his right, an upright shape that loomed forward. Then another, and another. He recoiled backwards as his rapidly dilating pupils realized that the space outside the iron doors were teaming with a host of enemies. He fell backwards, his hold on the syringe lost, it skittered across the tiled floor, his last hope failed. He scooted backwards on his behind, panicked, even as the large iron doors creaked open another inch, many eager fingers immediately slipped around the iron frames from outside to heave them open and admit the waiting throng. Makepeace got to his feet and turned and ran, through the teaching facility, banged into and sent trolleys and instruments flying in his path, he almost fell in his panic, arms a windmill to regain his balance, he fled.

# *Chapter XXIX*

*This I sat engaged in guessing, but no syllable expressing*
*To the fowl whose fiery eyes now burned into my bosom's core;*
*This and more I sat divining, with my head at ease reclining...*

Moran found himself once more sat upright in his hospital bed panting and trying to calm his pounding heart. This time he had no memory of the nightmare that had stalked him through his troubled sleep, but he knew that when he woke Ephraim had been there shaking him and trying to calm him. He leant back against the bed for several minutes until his respiration had subsided and then sat for a while in the darkened room, a single candle painting shadows across the walls. A troubling memory snagged against his mind. As Makepeace had turned with a promise of some hot calming tea, he had revealed, in the soft light of the bedside candle, a syringe, filled with a dark liquid, that was slipped quickly and stealthily into the man's pocket. For the briefest of moments Moran could swear he had caught a glimpse of a furtive and guilty expression painted across the man's graceless features. Was it possible that Makepeace would mean him harm? If so what would his motivation be?

He decided he had enough of this damned hospital bed, he was well enough, and bent down to the storage locker. He retrieved his trousers, coat and shirt but was shocked to discover that, while the shirt was dry, the coat and trousers were soaked through. He held them for some time, but no revelation struck him, so without better choice he slipped them awkwardly on, cinched the trousers as tight as he could, not finding any belt to fasten them properly. The bed slippers at his feet were soaked so even more puzzled, he looked under the bed and retrieved his shoes. His spectacles lay on the floor but when he bent to retrieve them he found them to be broken, so with a murmur of frustration he set them back on the locker and stood. Back in his own clothes, wet though they were, he felt himself once more. His confidence restored he extinguished the candle, plunged the room once more into darkness. He walked slowly down the hall and peered into Edgar's room. The patient was asleep, calm for once. He walked back down the long corridor toward the attendee's office, heels ringing against the tile. There was no sign of Makepeace, and the new doctor who was supposed to be assuming his own duties was asleep, his shoes on the desk. His face was hidden behind a gloomy treatise on liver failure in children, the face of a jaundice child on the cover comically replacing his own. On better days Moran would have taken pleasure in banging on the window to watch the junior doctor leap to his feet in fright, waiting for the shouted admonishment from his senior, only to see Moran creased with laughter on the other side of the glass, but Moran was too tired and simply shook his head and walked on.

Tired of languishing in a hospital bed, swamped in the sympathy of his colleagues he decided he needed fresh air, time to think and consider his options and actions. He walked through the echoing chamber of the vestibule, through the iron gates and into the cold rain of the courtyard. There was a man standing, unmoving in the shadows, watching the entrance. He was tall, familiar in some vague way. Moran shouted to him but received no response, the man neither answered nor moved, simply stared at the doors to the hospital. Moran took a step toward him, anger rising in his bones. The hospital grounds should be closed, secured against visitors and intruders. The tall man at last looked in his direction, acknowledged him and took a step towards him, hands supplicant in front. A boom of thunder and a flash of lightning, so close he could smell the ozone, broke the moment. Moran rubbed his eyes, the tall man had gone. He shook his head against the baffling and confusing events of the last few nights. He felt his heartbeat regularly in his chest, the lashing rain and the night air fortified him. The rain soaked him, dripped from his long beard but it felt good, refreshing compared to the confines of the hospital. Mason's park lay in front of him, a long detour to his home but he walked through the entry gates and walked home enjoying the feel of the rain and the sound of the wind in the leaves of the trees.

# *Chapter XXX*

*On the cushion's velvet lining that the lamp-light gloated o'er,*
*But whose velvet-violet lining with the lamp-light gloating o'er,*
*She shall press, ah, nevermore!*

Makepeace flung himself around the corner of the staircase and mounted the steps to the hospital's second floor, three at a time. Gasping for air he ran past the attending doctor's office, Donovan was still snoring in his sleep, journal over his face and the soles of his dusty and worn shoes crossed in front of him on the desk. Makepeace slid to a halt on the polished tile floor, filled with doubt. If the Cabal were inside the building would they limit themselves to Edgar's abduction or would they harm any others who could potentially harm or identify them. He decided to stick with his only plan and rescue Moran, and if there was time, Edgar to. He didn't know Donovan, and while he didn't want any harm to befall anybody but himself, he was certain time was short and there was only so much he could do before the Cabal reached the second floor. He slowed his steps and crept along the corridor to the patient's rooms. The door to Edgar's room was ajar, the curtains were open and the bed was bathed in moonlight. The recumbent form of Edgar Allan Poe asleep, unconscious perhaps, raving in the dreams of his delirium. Makepeace crept to the room next door and entered quietly.

"Doctor,' he whispered, "Doctor Moran, you must wake yourself. There is a great danger in the hospital tonight, evil walks its corridors. Wake up!"

Moran's room had the heavy drapes drawn closed and the room was pitch. With no response from the doctor, Makepeace tiptoed across to the bed. The sheets were piled on the floor, the bed was empty. He cracked the drapes to admit a sliver of moonlight to fall in an arc across the bed and the floor beneath. A patient's hospital gown lay there, discarded and crumpled, the locker opened and emptied, only the spectacles remained, lying broken on the cabinet. The Doctor had gone. Makepeace was confused, dumbfounded and uncertain what to do next. Time was fleet, slipping away as he struggled to process the hectic and confusing events of the night. Fingering the chain and the amulet in his fingers, slowly, ploddingly, a desperate idea crawled insect like into his brain. If he acted quickly, there was perhaps a small chance…

Fifteen minutes later Makepeace was running as fast as his sore and tired feet could take him, through the streets, south along Broadway towards Congress Court and the home of his only friend in the world, Doctor Moran. He could think of no other place the Doctor could have gone to after leaving the hospital in the middle of the night. But now, hidden beside the shabby brown stalks of a wintering hydrangea, outside the Doctor's home, he was filled with doubt. The house was dark and appeared unoccupied. No gas lights burned, no fire was in the hearth, no smoke came from the chimney. A gentle rain from the north soaked his clothes, made him shiver and tremble uncontrollably. A half hour passed, the rain was driving, freezing cold pellets against his skin, dark clouds raced low above him in the black sky. All traces of the earlier moon obscured. Full of doubt he crouched, wet and miserable, wondering where Moran could have gone at this time of night, in this weather. He was about to rise and walk away, leave this city forever, to escape the clutches and promises of the tall man when he heard heavy footfalls on the street beyond.

The jutting grey beard and bunched muscular shoulders of John Moran turned up the slick, rain shined driveway towards his house. John's mind was still confused, racing to catch up with the events of the last few days. The dream and the appearance of the tall man outside the hospital had thrown a stupor across his mind. He shook his head trying to clear the numbness from his thoughts. He reached for the key to his door when a harsh voice whispered from the shadows.

"Doctor Moran!"

Moran paused and turned slowly to face the voice. At first he could see nothing, the rain had intensified and dripped from his eyebrows and blurred his vision, vision already indistinct without his spectacles.

"Over here Doctor."

He saw the shape of a man step out incongruously from behind the row of hydrangeas in his yard. The man was stooped, thin shoulders hunched and shaking in the cold, his miserable face ungracious in looks and instantly familiar. Moran recalled the danger of the hidden syringe and checked his balance, ready for an attack if it was to happen.

"What is it Makepeace, what are you doing here. Speak now and tell me what you are doing at my home?"

"Oh, Doctor, please god, please help me. I have made a terrible mistake, I have fallen in league with the devil himself and this very night our hospital is under attack."

As he spoke Makepeace broke into tears, his arms hugged himself, pitiful in the cold rain that lashed across the night sky that drenched them both. Moran paused only for a moment.

"Come Ephraim, come into the house where we can talk without catching our deaths."

He turned the key with a shaking hand and with a sweep of his other he motioned Makepeace to enter before him. They entered the study together and Moran lit a candle and poured two large shots of cognac into his best crystal tumblers and sat, nodding toward a chair opposite for Makepeace to do the same.

"Now Ephraim, ordinarily I would send you away with a flea in your ear, and perhaps a call to the constables but I admit that this night has been beyond the ordinary. There are strange folks afoot and evil deeds being done, I admit that I am out of sorts myself and uncertain to what is happening," draining the cognac Moran filled his glass again, "so tell me Ephraim, tell me quickly and tell me true, what do you know of events this night and be sure to be as clear as this crystal of your part in them."

Ephraim needed a drink, his hands were still shaking, but he also suspected he would need his wits before this night was through so he placed the crystal tumbler, still full onto the small oak table between them. He leant his skinny frame forward and told Moran his story, his meeting with the tall stranger, the gold coins that sealed a contract implied. The threats in the alleyway the previous night, demanding entry to the hospital so that Edgar could be abducted and taken prisoner. He told his story up to the point of injecting Edgar with the phial and then racing into the Doctor's room to help him break loose of his nightmare, when Moran interrupted.

"So…the syringe was never meant for me?"

Makepeace was at once confused, shook his head.

"No. Never, Doctor, you are my friend. I would never do that to you," The interruption jogged his memory and he paused and reached into his pocket and placed the borrowed treatise gently onto the table in front of him.

"This was the only thing I brought from my home. It is precious to me although I must confess doctor that it was beyond me. To my shame I never did learn my letters."

Moran was instantly relieved, Makepeace had a myriad of faults, many of which bordered on the wicked, but he was an awful liar, "thank you for the return of the book. Once all this business is behind us we must take the time to teach you. So continue, what did you do next?"

"Forgive me Doctor, I tried and failed. I went down to the college wing thinking I might stop the tall man. I unlocked the door and…"

"What Makepeace? What happened."

Makepeace cringed into the shadows of his chair and his voice fell, crushed and defeated.

"There was an army waiting in the shadows."

Moran took a sharp breath and considered the news.

"So they have entered the hospital and have what they wanted. They have Edgar."

Makepeace squirmed in his chair. A strange look of guilty concern washed across his grey hooded eyes but simultaneously wrinkled the corner of his narrow mouth in a crooked grimace of knowledge of a hidden secret. Moran let out a long sigh and leant back in his chair in resignation of this night never having an end.

"What is it. What did you do Ephraim?"

"I hope that I did well Doctor. When I discovered you gone I panicked, time was against me and there was no help to be summoned from anywhere. I was about to run and abandon the hospital to the evil that I had permitted entry when a desperate thought came to me."

Moran knew from long years of experience that thoughts, especially good ones rarely presented themselves to the mind of Ephraim Makepeace.

"Please tell me Ephraim, tell me what you did?"

"I swapped the bodies."

"Bodies, what…which bodies. I am sorry Ephraim, I am terribly confused…but which bodies?"

It was Makepeace's turn to look puzzled, he shook his head and looked at the Doctor.

"Edgar's and Doctor Donovan's of course."

# *Chapter XXXI*

*Then, methought, the air grew denser, perfumed from an unseen censer*
*Swung by Seraphim whose foot-falls tinkled on the tufted floor.*

Moran sat in a stunned silence contemplating Ephraim's revelation. Such a simple soul, sat there in his darkened study, soaking wet and shivering, dripping rainwater onto the carpet. The world had not been kind to the poor man, his looks were harsh and his wits were slow but Moran had formed an unlikely relationship with him all the same. The news of the invasion at the hospital and the plot to kidnap Edgar, heaven knows to what end, was unsettling, but the news that the young doctor's life might have also been put in jeopardy, regardless of the good intentions was deeply troubling. The rain outside was still drumming against the window that looked out across the dark unlit lawns of his neighborhood. The street was asleep, not a single light was visible in the houses opposite. He stood to fetch a blanket and tossed it to Ephraim who wrapped it around his trembling shoulders. The candle on the table sputtered and cast creeping shadows across the hooked nose and downturned lips of his guest's face. He topped off his own glass with the cognac and let out a sigh, prepared himself for the rest of the tale.

"Tell me again Ephraim, tell me slowly and clearly, what did you do to Edgar and Doctor Donovan?"

"I was terribly hard pressed for time Doctor. I put a bolster in your bed, made it resemble a body and put the sheets back on the bed. The drapes I opened, just a crack so somebody in a hurry might look in the room and recognize that somebody, you Doctor Moran, were sleeping there. Seeing they were sleeping and no threat, they would move on without causing harm."

"I see, very good Ephraim, and then?"

"I went quickly to the attending Doctor's office and slipped inside without waking Doctor Donovan. He sleeps quite soundly as you may have noticed Doctor. Too many long hours I think."

Despite the circumstances, the faintest flicker of a smile stole across Moran's face. Makepeace had clearly been covering for the young doctor, probably taking on more work than he was responsible for to allow the doctor to get some rest. He remembered his days as a junior doctor and the ridiculous blend of grueling hours and burdensome responsibility.

"Yes Ephraim, it has been brought to my attention. I will look to find a means to reduce the hours we are making Doctor Donovan work."

Ephraim nodded a thank you, but a sheepish look stole across Makepeace's face as he continued.

"Forgive my sins Doctor, but as I say time was against me and my options few. I took the liberty of pouring a little chloroform onto a bandage and used it to…make sure the Doctor continued in his sleep."

Moran was once more stunned into silence. Ephraim squirmed in his chair while he waited for the doctor to shout, dismiss him from his position and throw him out of his house. In truth, Moran did want to stand and rant, but he also wanted the rest of the story and he wanted it quickly. He considered that the best way to get the story was to not upset or scare the storyteller. When Moran finally raised his head to speak, his tone was calm and he spoke kindly.

"So, you drugged Doctor Donovan. Good heavens, what else?"

"I wheeled him on his office chair down to the patient's room where Edgar still lay, unconscious and restrained. I placed Edgar in the chair and Doctor Donovan in his place, in the bed, put one of the leather anti-biting hoods we use for the disturbed patients over his face, secured his restraints, took his shoes and left."

"You tied one of our young Doctors to a patient's bed, masked him and then you took the man's shoes?" Moran was confused, "why, tell me Ephraim, why did you take the Doctor's shoes."

"Well, Doctor Donovan always slept with his feet on the desk. When I had wheeled Edgar back down to the Doctor's office and put Edgar in the office in his place, I loosely put his shoes on Edgar's feet and left them propped up on the desk in the same manner. Oh and the copy of the journal he was reading I placed over Edgar's face to conceal his identity. In that way, to someone in a rush and only giving a cursory glance, they might think the young Doctor was sleeping as usual and move on."

Moran couldn't stop shaking his head. The danger he had placed the young Doctor in was extreme, and yet he wondered if he would have acted with such creativity and acuity if he had been in the same position.

"Well Ephraim, I think we should return to the hospital you and I and see what we shall see. Perhaps there is a chance that the villains you describe could not, for some reason, carry out their nefarious deed, or perhaps Doctor Donovan was discovered and needs our assistance. Either way, we have a sick patient, uncared for and now wearing another man's shoes."

Moran stood, shook his head and looked down at the wretch opposite. Thin shoulders beneath the blanket, still shivering in soaked shirt and pants. Shoes barely strapped to his feet, his clothing a patchwork of coarse repairs and mismatched stitches.

"We are in need of haste Ephraim, but first I need dry clothes and we need to better dress you for the weather. Wait there."

He left the room and ran up the stairs to change quickly into dry trousers. He rummaged noisily in the closet for old clothes and soon returned with a pair of old boots, some dark corduroy pants and a white cotton shirt. A spare coat kept by the door completed the outfit and for the largest part was a passable fit. Ephraim stood, the shirt and coat hung off his thin shoulders but the shoes fitted snugly. He was suddenly overcome with emotion, at the unasked for kindness of the Doctor.

"Thank you…I really don't know what to say." Ephraim was close to tears and Moran was touched. The two men, not quite friends, but at that moment close enough, smiled at each other, a look that spoke across station and learning, opportunity and comfort. Moran's voice too was cracked with emotion.

"Come my friend, the night wastes and we have much to do."

Moran turned to leave when two shadows slipped across his window, shapes darker even than the ink of the night beyond. He motioned Makepeace to silence, and stepped lightly down the hall, lit only by a single flickering candle. The shadows at once loomed up against the leaded stain glass quarter panes of his door. One tall, the other shorter but broad. They loomed there for perhaps a minute before the door knocker was rapped loudly. Makepeace had crept down the hall to join the Doctor and lend his support, they both stood shoulder to shoulder wondering what more this night could bring.

Moran shrugged his shoulders and grabbed the hawthorn shaft of his walking stick and flung open the door. In the doorway stood the silhouettes of two men, Moran took a step backwards as they both stepped into his hall, the light from the candle finally reached their faces to reveal the bushy eyebrows and pointed beard of John Carter and the pale eyes, under the brim of a brown derby hat, set amidst the broad Slavic features of his accomplice.

# *Chapter XXXII*

*"Wretch," I cried, "thy God hath lent thee—by these angels he hath sent thee*
*Respite—respite and nepenthe from thy memories of Lenore…*

Moran had his stick raised, prepared to fight, and Volk had lowered himself to a crouch and begun to feint to his right in preparation for an attack when Carter held up his hand, an entreaty for peace.

"Perhaps, at this dark hour you will first allow me to introduce myself," said Carter, "if our presence still displeases you Doctor Moran, we will most certainly take our leave."

Moran was uncertain, but the use of his name made him lower the stick to his side although he still gripped the hawthorn shaft solidly in this right hand.

"Proceed then. Who are you and how do you know me?" Moran grunted.

"Doctor John Carter. You have heard of me I think. I did some business with your sister several years ago."

"That particular recommendation won't benefit you here sir. You were a cheat and a liar when you took money from my sister."

"A misunderstanding Doctor, given time I can explain, but our business here is pressing. We are here on behalf of Doctor Joseph Snodgrass. Does that name at least gain us entry to better plead our case for civility?"

Moran breathed out heavily while he weighed his options, but finally he stood aside and waved the two men through and into his study. He followed closely behind them and motioned them to take seats in front of the fireplace, cold but ready with tinder and fuel.

"Ephraim, would you be so kind as to make a fire for our guests?" he turned back to where Carter and Volk were seated, "and you Carter had best explain yourself and quickly! We have business ourselves this night and little time to spare."

Ephraim bent to light the fire and pretended to busy himself with the kindling while he listened to Carter's explanation of his encounter with William and Joseph in Richmond, the telegram summoning Joseph back to Baltimore and their subsequent journey onward to New York, Carter himself taking on the task to return to protect Edgar.

Moran dragged his fingers through his beard and nodded as the tale unfolded. The fire had begun to take flame, the kindling crackled and their faces were softly illuminated. Moran considered the events carefully. There was one thing that was still unclear in his mind.

"This William Walker you speak of I know not but I hope he is a reliable man. But you mention a telegram summoning Snodgrass back here. Who could have sent it?"

Carter looked up in surprise, he stared intently at the Doctor. He peered closely into his eyes for some time making Moran uncomfortable, but never broke contact.

"You did Doctor, though I perceive that you were and still are unaware. A magic has been enacted on you without your knowledge. It holds you still under its enchantment."

Carter turned quickly to Makepeace, who was still crouched by the fire warming his hands and pretending not to be listening to the conversation.

"And you. What is it that you are concealing? It reeks of power, it speaks to me. What is it?"

Makepeace rose from his place by the fire, his face flushed with guilt. Moran was confused and disoriented. He was certain he had sent no telegram and yet he had a sense of deep disquiet. What possible explanation could be offered to help explain his soaked clothing and slippers. If he had left the hospital at some time, where on God's tender earth had he been. The world seemed to have tilted several degrees from center. He felt dizzy with the gaps in his certainty of the events of the last few days. And now this wild accusation thrown at Ephraim! He needed to recover his senses and regain a grip on the situation that seemed to be spiraling away from his control. Moran rose to his feet, angry and perplexed.

"What are you talking about Carter? What do you mean an enchantment, and what exactly are you accusing this poor man of?"

"Please be seated both of you. I will try to explain."

Makepeace sat at once, his face crumpled with contrition and foreboding. Moran more reluctantly finally took his seat, he slumped into his armchair with a grunt, arms folded across his broad chest.

"There are dark and evil forces at work gentlemen, sorcery and magic are at play and demon's walk the earth tonight." Carter held up a hand to forestall Moran's objection, as he had started to rise from his chair at the notion of magic and demons. "Please Doctor, a moment to plead my case."

Moran settled back grumpily but waved Carter to continue.

"A proof is needed I think. Makepeace, is that your name?"

Makepeace nodded but kept his eyes down and avoided the stares from both Moran and Carter.

"Take your hand from your right pocket and place the contents in mine," he demanded holding out his hand.

Makepeace glanced at Moran, but Moran was, at least for the moment, willing to let this play out and see what was revealed. There was nothing he could do, nowhere left to run. Makepeace dug around in his pocket and reluctantly placed the silver amulet and chain into Carter's palm.

"Vade Retro Satana, get behind me Satan," he read as he examined the amulet. "This is no ordinary charm, this belonged to the sisters Doctor Snodgrass travelled to New York to visit, it would have been a great gift to one who needed it desperately."

Carter raised his eyes to glare into those of Makepeace who shuffled uneasily in his chair, wished he could vanish and spare himself the wrath of Doctor Moran and these strange men who had sprung unbidden and unexpected into his life.

"So explain yourself, how did you come by this rare and precious thing?"

Makepeace collapsed into the chair, trapped by the events, only the truth provided a means of escape despite the punishment and retribution he was sure would follow.

"I took it sir. I don't know why. It seemed fair to me is all."

Moran was furious, the color rose in his face and Makepeace wondered if the Doctor was about to have another seizure.

"You took it from whom?" He paused to rub his temples and shake his head but he knew the answer to his own question at once, "Edgar of course. You took it from a dying man, a man in our care…"

Carter objected at once.

"Regardless of the reason for its taking, the possession of the amulet has offered protection, perhaps where it was needed the most."

"What do you mean Carter," said Moran angrily, "what possible motive justifies the theft from a patient?"

"You have both been victims of sorcery, compelled to carry out deeds on behalf of a group of demon hunters who are here in the city. They seek Edgar and the creature that possesses him."

Ephraim remained sunk in his chair, terrified of the consequences of the theft, but the mention of the demon hunters frightened him even more.

"The tall man," he whispered, almost to himself but Carter leapt to his feet at the name.

"Yes! And you Doctor Moran, have you seen a tall man, a stranger who has approached you recently?"

It was Moran's turn to fall silent. Confusion still addled his thoughts but he sensed the truth in what Carter had claimed. There had been a tall stranger outside the hospital. The details he was still unsure of, but he knew that although he had retained no memory of sending the telegram, he was now certain that he did so.

"Why would anyone sending a telegram to recall Doctor Snodgrass to Baltimore be of benefit to this…group of demon hunters you claim are stalking this city?"

"It wasn't Doctor Snodgrass that they required. It was the talisman he carried, the secret sword," he weighed the amulet in the palm of his hand, "joined together with this amulet, they would have secured powers that could not be resisted. It was luck, or perhaps I should say fate that sent him and the sword away, to New York, and brought me back in his stead. Here Doctor, take it for a moment."

He held the amulet out and Moran reluctantly reached across and touched the silver chain and the perfectly circular amulet. The silver gleamed brightly in the firelight and his fingers slowly closed around its perfect form. As he did so a veil was slowly lifted from the recesses of his mind, revealed a room full of memories that had been hidden from him. The meaning of the nightmare on the flaming beach was revealed to him. The offer of his services for the secret to the cure he had sought his entire life. His soul in return for the lives of millions, the treatment for consumption a small price to pay. He felt a hand touch him on the shoulder. Carter was there, standing close, a sympathetic smile crooked on his lips.

"It was all a deception Doctor. Whatever they offered you, pure deceit and treachery. But the stars are in our alignment, fate has smiled and in the very nick of time we have uncovered their spells. Makepeace's act of taking the amulet from around Edgar's neck had provided him with protection; now that the lies have been revealed, you are both free once more."

Moran nodded, somewhat sadly. Ashamed and belittled by the deception he had been willing to enter into. But an anger also burnt deep within him. He had lived his entire life with honor, it was outrageous that he had been so easily tricked into shaming himself and bringing discredit on his name. He stood and looked across at Carter and then down at Makepeace. The strange man called Volk was still seated quietly and patiently, his colorless eyes reflected the dancing flames. A need for retribution, for the wrong that had been put on himself and Makepeace lit a flame of vengeance within him. He was eager for action and a chance to redeem himself and wreak havoc on those who had tricked him. He was certain now that Doctor Donovan's life and that of Edgar Allan Poe was in great danger. A sense of deep, dark foreboding descended upon him but at the same time he became stalwart, adamantine in his resolve for retribution against his enemies.

"To the hospital gentlemen. We are needed there at once, and may the devil, if he exists, quake in his boots at the news of our arrival."

Moran gave Makepeace a stern look of disapproval for his actions as they readied themselves to leave the doctor's house, but reached into his walking stick holder by the door and selected a heavy and short handled cane that more closely resembled a shillelagh than a walking stick. He held it out to Makepeace with a grunt of approval as he weighed its balance and heft in his hand.

"Take good care of this my man, I would wager you will need it before this night is through."

In return Makepeace nodded thanks and took the stick.

Moran opened the door but before he could exit, Volk pushed rudely passed. Moran was infuriated but Carter restrained him with a hand on his shoulder and a whisper in his ear.

"While we have him, let him go first, he is blessed with certain gifts."

Moran looked back, a quizzical look on his face, but

shrugged and acquiesced, and watched as Volk circled across the lawn, always moving but in a manner that quickly and thoroughly covered all exposed parts of his familiar neighborhood. He nodded from the shadows and they joined him under the sycamore tree on the edge of his neighbor's property. As soon as they grouped, Volk took off into the darkness of the night.

The three followed, they walked quickly together toward the hospital, Volk always slightly ahead and on the opposite side of the street. As they approached Broadway the shadow of the brick edifice of the hospital loomed in front of them, the iron gates were open but the courtyard was deserted. The rain had eased and a thin pairing of the moon slipped between the remaining clouds, alternately threw faint silver lights across the grounds before returning them to deep shadows. Moran wanted to proceed straight through into the great domed vestibule. He was impatient to check on the condition of both Donovan and Edgar but Carter held him back.

"From what you say, the attack would have come through the doors at the rear of the hospital. It is there we should look first to see if we can obtain clues as to what happened. Makepeace, lead the way please."

Makepeace looked terrified but hefted the club in his hand and slipped away from the group to skirt the entryway and lead the group around the path used by the orderlies and janitors to free the hallways for the patients and medical staff. A heavy bank of cloud had totally occluded the moon and the path was pitch black in front of his feet, but the way was familiar. A noise to his left startled him but when he peered into the gloom he could just make out the eerie pale eyes of the man they called Volk tracking his progress from the bushes away from the path. Finally the group rounded the hospital wing and entered an area not normally seen by the public or most of the staff. Large containers for refuse were lined up alongside the walls and other smaller waste bins were packed with medical waste, bandages and swabs, covered in the blood and filth of the profession. The space reeked of putrefaction and rats fled their arrival, squeaked in indignation and scurried to reach their nests hidden in the walls of the hospital.

# Chapter XXXIII

*Quaff, oh quaff this kind nepenthe and forget this lost Lenore!"*
*Quoth the Raven "Nevermore."*

The train came to a final halt with a woosh of steam and smoke that for a moment enveloped the train, blacked the windows and darkened the inside of the carriage. I swigged the remains of the coffee and we all stood, eager to stretch our cramped limbs and leave the train. I checked my pocket and touched the familiar shape of the Derringer. I only had one bullet left and had no time to seek out an armorer for fresh ammunition, but the touch of the cold steel still felt comforting to me. Despite the urgency we all felt, Darko held us back until the carriage was empty, then nodded and we disembarked, followed his careful lead. As we exited the station we were almost blown from our feet. The wind howled up Conway Street carrying heavy rain from the Atlantic. I shrugged my coat tight around my neck and wished once more, with a glance of resentment at Darko's back, for my elegant black topper, the one I had left behind, crushed in Carter's filthy cellar.

Evening was tumbling quickly across the rooftops of the industrial buildings that surrounded the station. The late afternoon light was already slipping away from us; it was a dreary Sunday evening in October and there wasn't a cab to ride as far as the eye could see. I almost cried out in frustration, turned to look around but the streets were empty. Darko grabbed my elbow and started to walk me briskly eastwards, up Conway Street toward the Inner Harbor from where we had started our journey four long days ago. We passed West Mulberry Street a few minutes later, I peered down the long street and could just make out the warm glow cast across the wet pavement from the windows of Martick's, windows already crowded with early diners. A hot lamb broth and a glass of wine rather than this desperate rush towards danger and terror. I paused for a moment, eager to cease this desperate crusade and take comfort in such a familiar place but Darko's had marched onward, resolute in his desire to meet with Carter, his outline receded into the shadows ahead. With a sigh I picked up the pace to catch him.

We joined Pratt Street close to the harbor, the wind snapped the rigging of the ships and jangled the chains against the flagpoles that marked the entrance to the pier. The tall masted ships moored to the pier were tossed and rolled in the heaving waves of the river, the hawsers taut against the mooring bollards that secured them. Rain lashed across the pavements in curtains and the clouds above us raced across the sky. The wind was against us and smelt of the ocean, it forced us to lean as we made heavy progress. Gas lighters strolled past us on the opposite side of the street, the gale making them unsteady on the small ladders they carried to reach the valves and light the gas lamps. We continued to scan the streets for cabs but the city had emptied, the streets forlorn and vacant.

So, still on foot we hurried, a punishing pace set by Darko, along East Pratt Street and across the small footbridge that spanned the narrow Jones Falls river that would empty into the Inner Harbor to our right. With each step the anxiety and tension increased. My heart pounded and my feet felt like lead, a dread fell upon me, a deep well of foreboding in the pit of my stomach. I searched the streets, foolishly hoping we might somehow stumble upon Carter and Volk but amidst the storm, our little band were the only souls foolish enough to be abroad. We marched five more city blocks and only stopped when the wide boulevard of Broadway lay across our path. A line of spiked iron railings wrapped the courtyard. The five storey brick edifice of the Washington College Hospital towered above us, the gold topped tower crowned by the iron cross of Christ reached into the racing clouds.

# *Chapter XXXIV*

*"Prophet!" said I, "thing of evil!—prophet still, if bird or devil!—*
*Whether Tempter sent, or whether tempest tossed thee here ashore,*
*Desolate yet all undaunted, on this desert land enchanted…*

Edgar woke slowly from a dreamscape that seemed to continue around him. His delirium had not abated and he was weak, so very weak. Fatigue washed across him, a vast ocean of ennui that stretched across the horizons of his mind. He opened one eye which pulled on the bandage across his forehead and made him wince. His eyes were covered by a paper, some kind of journal. He reached up and removed it, to reveal himself seated in a rolling leather chesterfield in a small cramped office of some sort. His legs had been propped up on the desk in front of him and shoes three sizes too large had been slipped loosely onto his bare feet. He was dressed in unfamiliar striped green and white pajamas, and not for the first time in recent days he realized he had absolutely no idea where he was.

He looked around for a moment or two. He felt lucid, for a moment able to think clearly. The dreams of recent days pushed back from his psyche. The ravens that pursued him, the cold plowed fields and skeletal trees of his nightmares a distant memory. He looked around to discover that in addition to the leather topped desk there were shelves overbrimming with medical books, and by the window, what looked like a coffee pot. He was parched and with some difficulty managed to swing his legs from the desk and reach up, only to find with disappointment that the pot was both cold and empty.

Carefully he eased himself to his feet. He was unsteady and light-headed, the room swung a lazy arc around him for a few minutes and he held onto the edge of the desk until it ceased its queasy movement. Sounds were muffled and he touched the bandages around his ears, confused as to their presence. He strained to recall the last solid memory, to place himself in a location, but his mind was an empty room bereft of furniture but with every corner filled with dust and cobwebs.

With his equilibrium returned he opened the office door and peered outside. The corridor was empty, although below him he could hear a disturbance, loud voices and harsh shouts. He shuffled along the corridor in his oversized shoes, the gas light made his shadow creep alongside him. He smiled at the sight of his shadow, so hunched, a grotesque old man his companion on this midnight foray to who knew where?

At the end of the corridor lay another, this one lined with doors. Halfway down this new corridor, one door lay open, a flicker of a flame from a candle cast moving shadows and shapes into the hallway outside. He shambled his old man's walk toward the light, dragged the shoes so they would stay on his feet. His progress was a slow meander and it took him several minutes before he stood outside the candle lit room. He hung onto the door jamb for several minutes more. The noise from down the stairs was increasing and his addled, tired mind struggled to make sense of what might be causing such a furor.

With a final surge of failing strength he pushed himself off the doorframe and took twenty teetering steps toward the window at the end of the room that lay open to the cold of the night. He wanted, desperately needed, to feel the night air on his face. He stepped in front of the candle and caught hold of the window frame to steady himself. The night outside was icy but he inhaled deeply anyway, the cold seared his lungs and made him cough but it centered his thoughts. The clouds flew above him, they streamed from the building behind him straight out in front, they soared, heavy with rain and storm towards the tiny lights of some town or city that lay beyond the canopy of the trees in front of him. A courtyard lay below, a vast tree in its center. A sycamore maybe or an old hoary oak, the weather too harsh to permit easy identification.

He eyes were heavy and his mind was beginning to wander once more, a journey back to the endless fields and rook and raven filled trees. He was about to turn and maybe take a small nap on the bed to his side when he thought he saw a tall figure step out from the dark shadows under the tree. It looked up, directly into his eyes. He could see no face but the way the figure stood and the manner in which it moved was instantly familiar. He was thrilled that the name came unbidden and with great familiarity to his thoughts and he whispered to himself, "Snodgrass," when something seized him from behind and he was lifted from his feet and swept irresistibly backwards into the room behind him. Darkness slipped across his gaze and a smile touched his mouth as he fell, downwards, returned gleefully to his madness.

# *Chapter XXXV*

*On this home by Horror haunted—tell me truly, I implore—*
*Is there—is there balm in Gilead?—tell me—tell me, I implore!"*
*Quoth the Raven "Nevermore."*

The tall spiked iron gates stood open before us, permitted unguarded entry to the courtyard. There was no sign of the gatekeeper, paid off no doubt, bribed to stay home and happy to do so on this awful night. Nevertheless, a portend of something untoward, something out of the ordinary was at large at the hospital. There was no sign of movement in the shadows that surrounded the entrance, although some gas lights were lit within, normally a sign of welcome and comfort to those who sought the refuge and healing of the hospital. Tonight they appeared ghoulish, the windows rendered to become yellow eyes in the building, staring out at us, a horde of hidden watchmen spying and poised, ready for our arrival. We stood in the rain for several minutes while Darko reconnoitered the exterior grounds. He finally returned, appeared silently at my shoulder causing me to jump and emit a curse. We were all tense, hoping beyond hope that we would find Carter here, together with Doctor Moran and Darko's physical manifestation of his alter ego, Mr. Volk. But there was no sign they had been here, the grounds were silent, still and waiting.

Darko motioned us to remain and slipped like a wraith through the gates. The shadows of the trees in the courtyard consumed him immediately. We waited in the almost shelter of some bushes, that had grown over the railings and hung like a canopy above us. He returned after only a few minutes.

"There are few clear signs to be read. Somebody stood under the large tree in the center of the courtyard for some time, the grass is still crushed there. There are many footprints, both coming and going, but the rain has destroyed any intelligence that could be gleaned."

I nodded understanding and as William himself had pointed out on the train, we had few alternative choices available, so we walked together through the gates into the courtyard of the hospital, apprehensive but ready for any attack that might come. I had my Derringer in my hand and I looked and saw that William was similarly prepared. Darko had no physical weapon, but he looked cocked and ready for any challenge, of this world or any other. There was no challenge from the shadows but the air was charged, electric with tension. Despite the driving rain that chilled our bones I found I was sweating and I had to change my grip on the pistol to stop it from sliding through my fingers. We moved slowly to stand under the large tree where Darko had informed us another had previously stood, and we looked together back up to the windows on the second floor. I pointed a finger at the window of the room where Edgar should be sleeping.

At first sight there appeared to be nothing untoward. Just the rows of windows, each marking the room of an individual patient. They were all dark save two. One was lit faintly by candlelight, the room next door had the curtains opened and faint light shone there but even fainter, possibly illuminated indirectly by light from the corridor beyond the patient's door. As we watched, searching for an indication of what lay ahead, something moved across in front of the flickering candle, temporarily darkened the room. There was a sharp gasp of excitement from William and then a face appeared at the window. It was difficult to discern through the rain that still swept in curtains across the courtyard, and the light from behind made a silhouette of his features, but I recognized the swept back hair, broad and still bandaged forehead of my friend, Edgar Allan Poe. He stood there for only a few moments seemingly taking in the night air, looking out across the trees to the city beyond. I took a step out of the shelter of the tree we still sheltered under and was prepared to shout when a large hand silenced me and pulled me back into the shadows.

"Wait!" spoke Darko, a menacing whisper in my ear.

We stood watching for a few moments and then a shout from the room broke the silence and Edgar disappeared. It was though he was pulled with some unimaginable force back from the window. I turned to look at Darko and at once he granted that the moment for action had arrived. Edgar was in some deadly peril, captured and held captive in his room. Darko stepped out of the shadows and sprinted for the iron doors that gave entrance to the vestibule.

# *Chapter XXXVI*

*"Prophet!" said I, "thing of evil!—prophet still, if bird or devil!*
*By that Heaven that bends above us—by that God we both adore—*
*Tell this soul with sorrow laden if, within the distant Aidenn…*

The rats scurried around the men's feet, panicked and desperate they ran over their shoes and made Moran shiver with revulsion at their touch. Makepeace took the rats in his stride and continued to follow the backs of Volk and Carter. Behind the large storage containers lay the two iron doors that gave entry first to the mortuary and then on to the hospital that lay beyond. As the men rounded the containers they were dismayed to see that the doors lay open, swung wide, abandoned. Carter withdrew a Colt Baby Dragoon Army pistol from his inside pocket and cocked the weapon as he approached from the side. He motioned for Moran and Makepeace to hold back and Volk slipped noiselessly across the open space, a specter in the shadows, to make his approach from Carter's flank. The two men walked up the steps that led up to the doors, steps laid to make the removal of corpses into waiting carts easier, and slipped into the darkness. Moran and Makepeace crossed the remaining space and stood shivering in the darkness, ears straining for any sound of a struggle.

Moran scoured the horizon for the sign of a distant dawn, but that promise lay hours away, the world rotating slowly west to east, time long diluted by the tension and threat of the violence they faced. There was only silence from within so they slowly climbed the stairs together and peered into the mortuary. Carter was visible on the far wall away from the open door, busy lighting a gas light. The flame guttered and flickered yellow and then took light, cast a ghastly green gleam across the gurneys that lay in ordered rows across the broad space. Some of the gurneys were occupied, cadavers waiting for disposal when the morning collection arrived. The gas light continued to grow and Moran could see that Volk stood at one of the gurneys looking intently down. He crossed the space quickly and joined Volk in his inspection. Donovan lay there, completely eviscerated. His intestines had been removed and still hung in gruesome coils of red and purple. Fresh crimson blood soaked the sheet he had been bundled in and his head lay to one side facing them, crudely separated from the stump of his neck. His dead eyes looked out accusingly, straight into the horrified grey eyes of Ephraim Makepeace who recoiled from the sight, hand over his mouth to stifle a scream. He smashed into the gurney behind him and sent a tray of surgical tools clattering noisily to the ground.

"Oh my poor soul, what have I done!" he shouted as he sank to the floor.

Volk bent down and silenced him with a strong hand across his mouth, strong but tempered with a measure of sympathy for the man's plight.

Carter walked briskly across to examine the remains.

"A sacrifice! See where the entrails have been removed the cavity is filled with ash. The removal of the head is also indicative of a ritual."

Volk bent to the floor and from under the gurney that carried the body he retrieved a leather ant-bite hood.

"If I read this correctly," spoke Carter quietly, "they transported the man they thought to be Edgar to this point. At that time, one of their ilk, one with half a brain, decided to double check that they were in fact abducting the correct person. The hood was removed to reveal our young doctor here. Their leader was furious and tortured this poor man in an act of vengeance."

"So where are they now, and where is Edgar?" asked Moran. He was repeatedly pulling his long beard, clearly distressed by the sight of the young doctor, but he still held the cane, the knuckles of his right hand white with the pressure of his grip.

"Once they realized their error they would have either fled or gone back inside to continue their search," said Carter, "my gut tells me that whoever, or whatever is leading them would not have given up so easily. They are still here."

Large double doors stood closed at the end of the room. Volk moved toward them and listened for several minutes before he slowly eased the right door open a slit and peered through the gap.

Moran took the opportunity to bend to the floor and comfort Makepeace who had rolled into a fetal position and rocked, his arms across his chest while he cried softly to himself.

"Ephraim. Oh poor Ephraim, there was no way you could have guessed that this would have been the outcome of your plan," Moran whispered, "you are not responsible for this. You are not responsible, but you can help apply some justice for the heinous act inflicted on this innocent man."

Ephraim's rocking slowed and finally ceased and he looked into the doctor's eyes. His grey pupils were red, raw with emotion. He continued to cry softly but was trying desperately to recover himself, to step back from the edge of madness and desperation that his action had pushed him towards.

"It *is* my fault, the blame *is* mine," he stated, simply but with finality, "however, I will help you avenge this man's life and pay the price for taking the amulet. For once in my pathetic frightened life, I will stand with the righteous side. I will help you and do what is within my power to avenge poor Doctor Donovan."

Moran wiped a tear of his own from his eyes and reached a hand down to Makepeace which Makepeace accepted, and with a grunt he hefted the man to his feet. Volk looked back and hissed a warning.

"They are coming and they are many, perhaps as many as fifty. A rag tag group of marauders led by a man, very tall."

He stood immediately back from the door and took a tactical position off to the right so that he could easily attack from the rear and close their exit. The double doors were thrown open and a man dressed in the manner of a harlequin ran into the room. He had painted his face to resemble a demon, red slits were painted horizontally across his eyes, and his mouth had been widened almost comically with the same paint. He had a broad and absurd grin of triumph on his face and he howled like a wolf as he sprinted in a straight line towards Carter. Carter fired a single bullet from his Colt which punched a perfect circle in his attacker's forehead. He was knocked from his feet and landed on his back, dead, the same grin stuck for eternity on his face. The remainder of the attackers paused, a dark press of anger crowded and hesitant in the dark space between the doors. They could be seen moving from side to side, eyes reflected the light from the gas lamp Carter had lit in the mortuary. Suddenly, there was a shouted command from the rear and the marauders attacked as one.

# *Chapter XXXVII*

*It shall clasp a sainted maiden whom the angels name Lenore—*
*Clasp a rare and radiant maiden whom the angels name Lenore."*
*Quoth the Raven "Nevermore."*

Darko entered the vestibule first, closely followed by William and then I. The broad space was empty, but signs of a forced entry were obvious. Broken glass was spread across the marble floors, chairs had been overturned and a small fire still burned weakly in one corner where a trash basket had been set alight. We began to climb the stairs to the second floor when a single gunshot rang out down the hall that led through the teaching wing and the morgue beyond. I was instantly caught between opposing emotions, snared between rescuing Edgar and investigating the fracas down the hall, I hesitated. William caught my arm.

"Let me help your friend like I did once before. If, with my life I can save him, I promise you I will." He looked me earnestly in the eye and nodded. He touched my shoulder, the touch of a dear friend and pushed me gently away and then sprinted up the stairs towards the patient's rooms. I turned to see Darko walking menacingly away in the direction of the fight and I resolved at once to follow him. I hurried my steps to catch him as he stalked down the tiled hallway, his heavy boots echoed from the walls that marked his approach. At the end of the corridor stood the double folding doors that led to the teaching wing. Darko never hesitated, he pushed boldly through and I followed. The sense of space was immediate, the vastness of the room palpable. Even darkened, the ceiling scaled into the heights of a dome above us, the walls opened up on either side. The only light that entered was from the far side. There, the doors to the morgue stood open, a light beyond spread an arc of faint illumination across the surgical trolleys and tables that formed an untidy labyrinth across the space. Clustered around the doors, a throng of bodies jostled and pushed to get through and into the morgue.

A figure stood apart at the rear of the mass of bodies. He was tall and was stood arms stretched wide, a silhouette against the light from the morgue. More and more bodies were heaving to get through the doors and attack what lay there. Their shouts were those of animals, fierce and feral. I stood at Darko's side marveling at the simple ferocity of the horde.

"Are they human?" I whispered, desperately afraid.

"Yes, mere flesh and blood. Slaves, chattels, animated and controlled by the being that stands behind them."

"And what manner of being is that?"

"I think you know Joseph, you have met one of their kind already."

"A Fury," I gasped in despair, "we have no way to defeat such a being without the sisters help."

"Now is not yet the time to lose hope Joseph. There are other things in this world that even Doctor Carter has not yet discovered."

"Carter?"

"Yes, if I am correct in my appraisal of the situation, it is he that the marauders are intent upon in their anger. He and Volk, my brother, lie behind the doors."

# *Chapter XXXVIII*

*"Be that word our sign of parting, bird or fiend!" I shrieked, upstarting—*
*"Get thee back into the tempest and the Night's Plutonian shore!*
*Leave no black plume as a token of that lie thy soul hath spoken!*

Volk had described them as "rag tag" and so they were. Deluded disciples of a conjuror or sorcerer, a mix of men and women, an odd joining of classes and stations, all dressed in a strange and discordant assortment of clothes. Some appeared to have dressed for a social occasion, others arrived from a job of labor. One thing that unified them was that they all wore face paint like the dead harlequin, smears of red and yellow paint daubed their hands and faces, crude imitations of what they believed a demon or devil might resemble. Flags and black pennants hung from their ragged clothing, they fluttered behind them as they ran. They carried few weapons, a knife here, an antiquated musket or rusted sword, but mostly unarmed. Still they continued to crowd into the morgue. Their leader held back in the shadows, a tall sinister shape against the blackness of the unlit training ward.

The marauders were vacant eyed but ferocious, their rapacity for violence could be felt across the room. Wild shouts and yells filled the air as they continued to spill into the room. Only the barrier of the door and their own animal hatred slowed their approach. If they had retained some semblance of humanity and organized, they would have already overwhelmed the small band of defenders. Still, pure numbers were against them and they continued to quickly bear down on the men. Carter didn't hesitate, as soon as the first throng entered the room he fired his revolver into the mass of the crowd. A woman screamed, a high pitched shout of agony as she threw a hand up to cover the wound in her neck that jetted arterial blood high into the air, she crumpled slowly to her knees. The throng paused for a moment, at once uncertain, but the tall man at their rear shouted a command, his voice harsh and strident and they renewed their attack, driven on by a greater power or a terror that compelled them forward.

"Spare them if you can," shouted Moran, "they are enchanted, just ordinary people misled and deceived into believing in an evil cause. They deserve our pity, not death."

"We are massively outnumbered Doctor, what do you suggest?" said Carter.

"Their leader conducts them from the rear, it is he we must defeat. Incapacitate them if you can but try not to cause any deaths."

Carter looked incredulous but shouted across to Volk.

"Spare them if you can Mr. Volk."

Volk looked back, his face a blank, unreadable, he shrugged noncommittally, but when the first attacker came within his reach he spun and delivered a kick to the man's kneecap that dropped him to the ground, still alive but rolling in agony. Carter fired his revolver and shot two more of their vanguard, dropped them to the floor holding leg wounds. Volk leaped into the fray, sent crushing blows to temples and ribs. The attackers were infuriated by his presence in particular and swarmed towards him, gnashed their jaws and reached with sharp nails to tear at his eyes. Volk was a maelstrom of violent proficiency. The added challenge of non-lethal force seemed to inspire him. He fought like a dervish, spinning and leaping, aimed kicks at knees and fists at elbows. He swept legs from under his attackers and easily blocked clumsy punches thrown in his direction. The marauders were common men and women, inexpert at violence and Volk was more than adept in his capacity for causing harm.

It was well that the attackers focused their energies on Volk. It left Makepeace and Moran on the edge of the attack, where they could dispatch the occasional attacker with blows from their sticks. The horde centered only where the tall man concentrated. It meant that the defenders were successful in picking off individual marauders without taking much harm in return. Carter jumped onto a gurney and was expert with the pistol, picked off the few armed marauders. One man, dressed in the black flowing robes of a priest sprinted towards him, a scimitar raised above his head. He yelled obscenities as he ran, swung the blade that whistled through the air. Carter kicked one woman who was attempting to climb onto the gurney to unseat him, hard under the chin, sent her sprawling back into the crowd while he simultaneously shot the priest in the shoulder, sent the scimitar spiraling through the air.

Without pause the attackers poured, unstoppable through the doors, they slowly, inexorably pushed the defenders back towards the iron doors at the rear of the morgue. At one point even Volk lost his footing and four attackers immediately fell upon him. Carter shouted a protest but seconds later Volk regained his footing, and though he bled badly from a bitemark on his neck, he beat his attackers back, delivered punches and blows with devastating speed, broke ribs and fractured any arms that reached for him. A pile of bodies, some unconscious, others screaming in pain from their injuries, created a wall in front of him that further impeded and slowed the attack.

Still, by pure numbers, the defenders were becoming overwhelmed, taking damage and soon found themselves separated. Carter was finally pulled by many grasping hands from the gurney and was quickly overpowered, he disappeared under a mass of teeming bodies. Makepeace and Moran had their backs to the wall of the morgue, flailing their sticks and striking skulls, but wherever one attacker fell another took their place. The marauders were fueled by an unnatural vitriolic rage, they screamed and howled, a frenzy of hatred. They would soon overpower and decimate their enemies, Moran gasped for air, despaired as he swung his club again and again. He felled one large brute of a man with a blow to his skull and in his place a pretty, but blank eyed young woman leapt at him, screaming, teeth bared, saliva dripped from her slack jaws as she reached to rake nails across his face to maim and blind him. Moran backed up in a panic but his back struck the wall. He threw the hawthorn stick in front of his face for protection. She clawed at the barrier, howled in a frenzy of hatred and frustration. She was wild and raging. Spittle flew into his face and her teeth snapped at his nose and lips as she pushed forward in her rage. Moran despaired at last and closed his eyes against the attack. Suddenly he felt her weight slide to the floor. Makepeace had fought his way back to the doctor just in time and struck the girl from behind, to fold her knees. A large red faced woman dressed incongruously in an evening gown took her place and Moran swung hard, hit her on the temple with the heavy silver pommel. He struck her a concussive blow and she should have fallen, but instead she stood stock still in front of him, expensive pearls around her ample neck, stared, silent and unseeing. The rest of the room too had fallen silent. Moran pushed her out of his way and saw that the attackers had all stopped in their assault.

They appeared now as sleepwalkers woken rudely from a midnight pillage of the kitchen. They looked around themselves, confused, bewildered at their situation. They staggered, bumped into one another, no longer fueled by the animosity and malevolence that had ensnared them. They looked down in dismay at those fallen at their feet. One woman brushed her hands down her clothes as if to remove some unseen dirt. Another, a short man dressed like a sweep spun in a slow circle, stared at the walls and contents of the morgue, baffled at his predicament. Those that were injured were the most pitiful, they held broken wrists and nursed fractured arms, nonplussed expressions across their bruised faces. Open mouthed and slack jawed, some missing teeth and bleeding profusely from facial wounds, those that could walk all began to shuffle and stumble solemnly towards the open doors at the end of the morgue, climbed painfully down the steps outside and disappeared into the cold wet night.

Carter tried with difficulty to get to his feet. His clothing was shredded and he had an open wound across his forehead and deep teeth marks across his right forearm. His pistol was missing and his face was ashen but he managed to stand and take time to check on the health of the others. Moran was bent over holding his knees, gasping for oxygen. Makepeace had fared better, he still held the bloodied shillelagh in front of him, wary of the silent mass that walked slowly and eerily past him. Volk had already recovered and was walking quickly across the floor of the morgue, stepped over unconscious bodies towards the doors to the teaching wing. In the space between the doors stood the tall man, and behind him he could see his brother balanced on the balls of his feet, arms raised and fists coiled into boulders. The tall man had uncoiled a long dark whip and Darko was already bleeding profusely from a deep cut across his cheek.

# *Chapter XXXIX*

*Leave my loneliness unbroken!—quit the bust above my door!*
*Take thy beak from out my heart, and take thy form from off my door!"*
*Quoth the Raven "Nevermore."*

Darko began to move at once and I followed, matched his fast stride. There were only a handful of attackers left and they quickly dispersed through the doors as we approached. The Fury had its back to us, it was singularly intent upon its purpose, focused on the control and manipulation of the band of marauders it orchestrated. It chanted an incantation and at the end of its outstretched arms its fingers circled, formed the shapes that created the invocation of control that drove its followers to evil and violence beyond the doors. Darko strode briskly, quickly closed the gap between us and the Fury. Together we closed to within thirty feet of the beast when he suddenly came to a stop, held out an arm to bar my progress.

He looked across at me and gestured to the Derringer in my hand.

"Doctor Snodgrass, if you would be so kind?"

The sound of battle from the morgue rose in pitch, the battle seemed to be going badly for us, the raider's shouts of excitement had intensified. Every moment we delayed meant more harm might befall our comrades so without question I raised the little pistol, aimed carefully for the back of the creature's skull and without pause squeezed the trigger. The discharge was deafening and the sound echoed hollowly around the empty room. Once more the bullet flew a little high but struck the creature solidly in the back of the head. I witnessed a puff of red mist and a cloud of black hair fly from the impact point. The creature took a step forward to regain its balance from the impact. The noise of the battle ceased immediately. A flap of skin hung from the creature's scalp. Slowly it lowered its arms and turned to face us. The bullet had not penetrated its skull but the blow had dislodged one of its eyes. It hung on a sinew that still attached it to the orbit of the skull and rested wetly on the cheek of the beast.

It glared with open disdain at us, and reached behind with its right hand to withdraw the coil of a whip from a belt tied at its hip. The loss of the eye impeded its acuity, so while it let the tail of the whip drop to the floor, with its left hand it reached up and behind its head to seize the flap of skin. It pulled hard and stripped the flesh from across its skull. The face slipped noisily from its face, a wet bundle of blurred features in its hand which it let drop to the floor at its feet. I felt the bile in my throat rise at the sight and wondered darkly who the man had been, the donor of its skin and face that it had cravenly worn to deceive. Who had he been, what dreams and aspirations he had entertained, and in what monstrous, lonely way had he died.

Like its sister, it now stood revealed, yellow skin stretched taut across a large skull, it continued to stare from the sunken pits where its eyes should have been. Finally it opened the cavity of its maw, revealed its black and pointed teeth and let out an earsplitting scream, a howl of enmity in our direction. Terror bristled the hair on my back and arms and I took an involuntary step backwards. Nausea swept through me, dread nailed my feet to the floor and numbed my muscles but Darko was unmoved, he faced the creature, stoic in his resolve to confront and kill the creature if it was within his power.

The Fury slowly and deliberately unraveled its whip. The whip was twenty feet in length, made from twelve intricate plaits of dark oily black leather. It tapered to a fine point where the twelve plaits became separated. To each of the twelve strands a black iron spike the shape of a talon was threaded, sharp and brutal and designed to rent and tear the flesh of any creature it touched.

"I name you Tisiphone." Said Darko, his strange Eastern European accent somehow fitting for this moment, an echo from a more ancient world. "Denizen of Hades, return to the underworld. You have no place here."

His voice was loud and commanding but the Fury ignored him. It took a step towards us and let the tail of the whip snake like a menace across the floor. The black talon's clinked and sparked across the polished tiled floor.

"We have already killed your sister. Megaera is dead. Return before you share her fate and join her in hell."

When Darko spoke the name of the beast's sister the Fury flew into a blind rage. It advanced on Darko, hissed and spat animosity as it unfurled the whip and lashed at him. The whip snaked through the air, a whistling coil that accelerated and cracked a threat towards him. He took a defensive step backwards and began to raise an arm, but the barbed tails of the whip were moving faster than the speed of sound and one of the talons caught him across his right cheek. He gave no indication of his injury, he continued to glare at the creature as it drew back the whip for another strike, dark crimson blood flowed freely down his face and fell to form a pool on the floor. At that moment the bulk of Volk crashed into the creature's back, sent it staggering forward three steps. Darko was now close enough to strike and he sent a hammer blow of an uppercut to the creature's jaw. It shook its head but appeared unhurt and recovered instantly.

Now the three were caught in a delicate and deadly dance. Darko and Volk feinted and parried, circled the Fury in a coordinated ballet. The whip lashed again and again, sometimes missed, the barbed ends tore at the floor or cracked loudly in the air too close to their faces and arms, but more often than not, made a tearing and brutal contact. The men counterattacked when they could. Crushing blows to the creature's arms and ribs, but the Fury seemed oblivious. The dance continued, feint and dodge followed by strikes and brutish kicks. The Fury spun and leaped in the center of the attack, the tail of the whip in continuous motion, cutting the air and landing pitiless blows.

For several minutes the fight was well matched, the animosity and hatred of the creature balanced by the native competence of the brothers but soon it became apparent that the two men were slowly losing ground. Cuts and gashes appeared on their faces and bodies as they dodged and then tried to slip within the strike of the whip to land a blow. The creature was agile and supernaturally swift. The whip cracked and snaked through the air to land strike after strike. Blood seeped from many wounds and the two men, men I believed until that moment to be unbeatable, indomitable, were gradually but insistently becoming exhausted. Their dance began to lose its brisk cadence, their surety slipped, footwork faltered and they began to miss with their aim, blows landed with less harm.

I saw Carter, Moran and Makepeace enter from the mortuary. Like me they stood transfixed, horrified as Darko and Volk were slowly torn to pieces in front of them. We saw Volk take a vicious blow across his chest, six parallel lines of blood opened across his shirt and he staggered back, almost fell to his knees, his eyes wide. The creature howled in victory and advanced on Darko who was stood, holding a hand across his right shoulder where most of the flesh appeared to have been stripped from the bone and sinew beneath. He was breathing heavily, panting from the pain and exertion, close to finished, exhausted and finally defeated. He looked across the space towards Carter and Volk who stood behind the creature. He nodded, a silent command and then stood tall in front of the Fury that towered over him.

"No!" I shouted across the space that separated us, but the creature didn't pause, the whip cracked and the talons snaked once more through the air and wrapped around Darko's head, the talons snagged his eyes and ripped the flesh across his face.

Volk understood the sacrifice, the two were mentally entwined and he had instinctively anticipated the only act that could provide a winning outcome. He was already sprinting when the whip was taken back for the strike and when the black iron talons landed so did he. He leaped into the air and landed heavily on the creatures back, coiled his strong legs around its midriff and thrust one arm around its neck. The creature thrashed and bucked but Volk held tight. He looked back over his shoulder and Carter threw something towards him, it sparkled in the air as it fell end over end. Volk deftly caught it and immediately looped the silver chain around the creature's neck, the hard silver amulet hard against its esophagus. He grasped the chain underhand around the base of the fingers on both hands and using the leverage of his legs leant back, exerted his entire and considerable strength to strangle the writhing, raging beast.

A normal silver chain should have broken and I recognized that this must be the final talisman, the charmed amulet, given to Edgar for his protection by the Fox sisters. I had no idea how Carter came to possess it but hope shone at last. The chain flamed orange and yellow, then burst into a blaze of pure white energy. The Fury screamed in agony and frustration. It convulsed and thrashed around the room. It dropped its whip to prise Volk's hands from their grip on the chain that burnt its way into its neck, but the man was beyond defeat. Volk's hands were not immune though, smoke billowed from his palms and he threw back his head in a rictus of agony. The smell of burnt meat and singed hair filled the room. But he held on tight and continued to saw the chain brutally into and across the creature's neck. Finally, the creature's wild convulsions slowed and it fell to its knees. The Fury let out a croak of a scream from its crushed throat. The chain shone its brightest, a conflagration of white fire that blinded those of us that watched in shock and horror, but also with faint hope, then the light died down, faded to black, its light forever extinguished.

Volk fell to the ground, he stared blankly, in shock at

his hands. All of his fingers were missing, seared from his hands by the heat of the blaze that had also killed the Fury. Only the thumbs and stumps remained, blackened and charred. He looked across at his brother in dismay to see him staring sightlessly from empty eye sockets, a harsh and cruel line of flesh stripped in a line across his face.

# Chapter XL

*And the Raven, never flitting, still is sitting, still is sitting*
*On the pallid bust of Pallas just above my chamber door;*
*And his eyes have all the seeming of a demon's that is dreaming...*

We all avoided approaching the body of the Fury with the exception of Carter who bent to inspect the amulet. He retrieved it carefully from where it hung around the creature's neck and then juggled it from palm to palm until it cooled sufficiently for him to bear its touch. It had burnt to a matte black coal, a bare nugget, no sign of the rare and precious silver and delicate engraving remained to be seen. The chain was brittle charcoal, but he put in his pocket nevertheless, reluctant to let such a prized talisman be left behind.

I moved to Darko's side and Moran walked over to take care of Volk. Darko's eyes had been ripped cruelly from the sockets, he was completely blind. After checking Volk's condition for a few minutes, Moran stood and walked over to me and placed his hand on my shoulder.

"My part in this battle is over Joseph, I admit, I am no soldier. Let me stay behind and help these poor men. There are bandages and ointments sufficient in the college wing to at least ease their agonies and stifle any infection."

I nodded my agreement. The smell of the burnt flesh still filled my nostrils, repulsed, I felt dizzy and cold. I recognized the symptoms of shock, a reaction to the combat and violence we had all witnessed. I placed my hand on Darko's shoulder and he turned his face to mine. I suppressed a gasp of horror at his ruined mien. He was in considerable pain but sat calm and still, patiently waiting for Moran to finish helping his brother.

"Thank you," I said simply.

"In my country, my name means 'gift'. I was happy to give it to you Doctor Joseph Snodgrass." His voice harsh, spoken between teeth gritted in agony but he continued speaking calm and levelly.

"Don't let the giving of my gift be in vain my friend. Work remains to be done this night."

"But the battle is surely won?"

"Always assume one more enemy lies in wait."

I wondered at the meaning but before I could ask, Moran came across to assess his patient and administer a vial of morphine into his arm. Darko fell silent and would, or could not say any more.

Moran and I raided cupboards and lockers and piled sufficient supplies to patch the most urgent wounds. While Moran focused on Darko and Volk I applied a tincture of carbolic acid to the gash on Carter's forehead and the bite wounds on his forearm. Makepeace had survived relatively unscathed but I bathed the scratches he had received on his face and arms. I had to physically turn his head to effectively treat him, he couldn't take his eyes from the corpse of the slain Fury that still knelt, head hung forward on its charred and ruined neck. When I finished, he immediately turned back, walked across to the recumbent form and kicked with all of his strength, strength bolstered by guilt and horror, knocked it to the ground. He spat coarsely on the corpse and turned back to face us. Moran paused for a moment in his work.

"Will you lend me your help Ephraim?" the doctor asked kindly.

Makepeace thought for a long time. It was clear that he wanted most to help the doctor. To apply what mending he could to our friends and saviors, but at last he looked back at the doctor.

"No, not yet Doctor Moran. I stole the amulet from Mr. Edgar and opened the hospital doors, sending Donovan to his doom. I will follow Doctor Snodgrass, if he will have me. If the poor man needs help I will help him if I can."

Moran nodded, satisfied with the answer and turned back, busy with his work. With that we came together in a small group, me, Makepeace and Carter. We left the college wing together and walked mournfully back down the black and white tiled corridor in the direction of the atrium and the stone stairs that would lead us to the second floor. I felt vaguely naked without either Darko or William by my side and my thoughts immediately sought out William and wondered if trouble had found him in Edgar's room. My earnest hope was that Edgar was still alive and William had managed to find him and keep him safe from the tumult we had faced. We quickened our pace and mounted the stairs quickly, only paused at the top to listen carefully for any sight or sound of a threat.

The second floor corridor was silent. Along the corridor only a single door lay open, the light from the candle we had seen from the courtyard still burnt, flickering shadows danced in the corridor outside the door.

"William?" I half shouted half whispered.

"Joseph! I am glad to hear your voice. Come here, all is well."

# *Chapter XLI*

*And the lamp-light o'er him streaming throws his shadow on the floor;*
*And my soul from out that shadow that lies floating on the floor*
*Shall be lifted—nevermore!*

We all immediately relaxed, shared smiles and strode confidently down the corridor towards William's friendly and welcoming voice. I felt elated, keen to see Edgar at last, a vast weight lifted from my shoulders. The dark plot vanquished, its leader, the seemingly indomitable Fury defeated. We had suffered casualties certainly, but Moran was a skilled healer and he would offer what succor he had. I had even started to think of breakfast at Martick's at the end of this endless night. And so it took me several moments to process the scene when we arrived outside Edgar's room.

The window lay open to the elements, the drapes were billowing, snapping into the room, caught by the wind that drove cold rain across the bed and floor of the room. Outside it remained black, the clouds still raced in the sky and obliterated any sight of the moon. William was standing, his back to the wall, facing the window. His clear and honest expression beamed, a broad smile of welcome as we entered. His blond hair had fallen across his azure blue eyes that twinkled behind the frames of his spectacles that had, once more, slipped down the bridge of his nose. All appeared as it should with the exception of the long razor that he held under the throat of Edgar Allan Poe.

Edgar was slumped, oblivious in its grip, eyes open but unseeing. The razor was pushed hard across his Adam's apple, a bead of crimson blood rested on the shining edge of the blade. Carter was the first to recover his senses, he shook his head sadly.

"Darko shared his suspicions with me but I chose to ignore him. I regret that now."

William laughed, but his voice had changed, the clear

friendly tone I had become familiar with, replaced by a harsh slide of gravel that pricked my skin. I was, I admit dumbfounded, slack jawed I stared at the man I thought to be my friend, my accomplice in this matter.

"Cat got your tongue Snodgrass?"

He cast the words at me, flung venom and hatred and I stepped back away from the unexpected enmity.

"But…but you are my friend." I managed to say, realizing how childish and naïve it must have sounded even as I spoke the words.

"I was never your friend you fool. So easy to deceive, so desperate to be liked, so eager for company and fellowship. For a thousand years I have existed. The torture and deception of man has long been my dominion, but never have I met someone so wretched and desperate for comradeship as yourself Joseph."

He spat my name, a curse on his tongue.

"But you rescued Edgar. It was you who found him."

He laughed again, a screeching sound that keened, the wail of a beast.

"I had pursued this wretch for days. The charms he carried had obscured him from my senses. Until I fell upon him, almost by accident, in the alley outside that cursed Tavern in the seventh ward. It was there that I found him, dressed like a fool in his straw hat and miner's clothes. The witches had done well, even then he almost slipped by me. But the act of the concealment also revealed. The sword spoke my name as he walked by, it called out to me in terror and exposed the one who bore it. He cowered before me, a madness was already upon him, and when I stepped out of the alleyway and revealed my true form, he fell to the gutter unconscious. At long last I had him and could take possession of the demon he carried. That's when the fat landlord interfered with my plan, he shouted out to me, thinking me some common rogue and I was forced to come up with my deception. Still I knew from the moment I met you Snodgrass, that it would be you who would end up giving him to me."

"Why not stay in Baltimore and take what you desired?' Asked Carter.

The creature hissed at Carter.

"Because what I desired was the demise of you and all that you stand for Carter. You and the destruction of the witches was what I coveted beyond all else. And this ignorant wretch," he motioned towards me, "gave me everything, even the secret realm of the sisters, long hidden and greatly sought after. I could afford to take my time, follow this fool from Baltimore to Richmond, to New York, revealing all of my enemies for me, one by one."

"But if you are not William, who…what are you?" I asked. My voice broke, too high in pitch. I sounded like an infant. One scolded and ignorant, all of my actions, from agreeing to and allowing William to accompany me to Richmond, to finding the witches lair and inviting him inside, thrown back at me, showing me to be what the creature called me, a fool, a wretch, gullible and guileless.

"This is Alecto, the last of the Furies Doctor," spoke Carter kindly.

Hearing its name, and being called the last, the creature holding Edgar, roiled within the skin it had adopted as its own. It removed the razor from Edgar's throat but still held him cruelly. It reached up with the razor, and from the scar at the parting of its fair and blond hair, slowly cut a long line across its forehead. It pulled the skin down across its face to reveal its true identity. The blood of the man it had slaughtered for its deceit, dripped down its eyeless face and streamed into the maul of its open mouth. The yellow tinge of its skin was tight across the hard bones of its face. It discarded the ruined face I had grown so familiar with, without care, the man it had once been cast aside.

"You killed your own sister," I said, aghast.

The creature bared its black and jagged fangs at me, a

snarl of detest.

"At the end you left me no choice. I had spilt my own blood, a blood sacrifice to set flame to the orb and allow Megaera to overcome the witches. She had nearly defeated them when that abomination Darko entered. He gave them sufficient time to recover and mount a counterattack. With Megaera held captive between the deep mystery of the mirrors, her death was fated. To survive I was left with no other choice but to protect my identity as William Walker and slay my own sister."

The Fury renewed its grip on Edgar, tilted his head back with the force of the razor at his throat. Blood flowed freely from the cut as the razor pierced his skin.

"And now, I will exact vengeance on all of you for that deed and finally take possession of the demon!"

Makepeace had remained silent through the exchange, he stood close by my side. I could feel him tremor with fear as he faced the creature. As the razor's lethal edge sliced through Edgar's parchment skin, Makepeace launched himself at the Fury. He grabbed the hand that held the razor in an attempt to keep it from its killing motion. The creature released Edgar and he slipped to the ground, a line of drool from his open mouth ran into the growing stain of blood on the neck of his pajamas. The creature took hold of Makepeace's face and threw the man back across the room to land heavily at the base of the wall. He lay stunned and held an arm out in front him, the bone of a compound fracture pierced the skin. He reached up to try to rise and inadvertently took hold of the corner of the hessian green bedspread that still lay carelessly draped across the face of the polished steel mirror. As he tried to rise, his weight on the bedspread pulled it away to reveal the shine of the steel that reflected the soft light of the blue hour, the very first touch of a pale new dawn that finally peeked across the canopy of trees in the courtyard.

The Fury reached down and grabbed Edgar by the hair and began to swing the razor, an arc that would cleave through his throat, kill him and release the demon trapped within. As the blade descended, Margaretta stepped out of the depths of the mirror at its back. Her long jet black hair framed her pale face. Her black pupils filled her eyes, and they blazed retribution and destruction as she plunged the serrated iron blade she had taken from its sister deep into the monsters back. She twisted the blade and the Fury howled and tried to step away from the agony of the thing that impaled it. Margaretta stepped forward to maintain the pressure and the Fury opened its mouth and let out an endless shriek that shook the walls.

Edgar had slipped once more to the floor but as I looked, his eyes opened. His expression was peaceful and entirely lucid. He looked puzzled and covered his ears reflexively at the sound of the creature that stood in its agonies above him. He looked upwards and saw me, a wistful look passed across his face. The demon within him, sensing that its hosts life was ending slipped from its self-imposed shackles. A shape appeared on Edgar's back, small at first, the size of a small child but bird like in its movements. It crawled and scurried across his back and climbed to his shoulder. Its dark yellow eyes shone in the dawn's first touch and it scanned the room, eager for escape, seeking out a new host. It sensed both the power of the Fury and also its agony, and for a few brief moments its susceptibility to attack and domination. Raum's raven visage darkened with eager intent. The Fury contorted and convulsed on the blade, still screeched open mouthed, and the demon on Edgar's back slowly spread its iridescent wings. It took flight beating its wings loudly in the small space, it circled the room, forcing Carter and I drop to the floor to avoid its touch. The raven circled to the top of the room and flew directly at the Fury that howled mouth wide in a rictus of agony and frustration. The bird flew straight at the creatures open maw, sensing its weakness, knowing it was vulnerable for the first time in its thousand year life, to attack and possession. The bird entered the mouth of the Fury and vanished.

The Fury writhed and screamed in an attempt to repel the demon from its being, but it was hampered and weakened by the wound and the presence of its own sister's knife against its spine. The struggle continued for only moments, its skin rippled and convulsed as Raum exerted its will and dominion over the mind of the Fury. As Raum began to dominate, the beast fell silent and Margaretta stepped back, pulled the black iron blade, blood slicked from the beasts back. It retained the wits to at once turn and reach for her but she was fast and slipped easily out of its grasp, stepped to the side of the mirror she looked me straight in the eye and spoke directly into my thoughts.

"Now, dear…sweet Joseph. Do it now."

I knew exactly what to do, and without hesitation I rose from the floor and took two brisk steps forward. With all of my might I pushed the Fury, and the demon that had taken possession, through the portal that Margaretta had opened and into the deep mysteries of the steel mirror.

Margaretta immediately dropped the iron blade, it was filthy and vile to her touch and it clanged and clattered on the floor. She didn't speak a word, perhaps she had passed beyond the realm where human speech was needed. Her pupils had dilated, they shone in the growing light of the new day, she brushed the hair from her eyes and at last she smiled, sadly but with kindness. Happy for those who had survived but mournful for the loss of life and limb and precious charms, lost forever from the world. Her raven hair flowed in the breeze from the window and she looked me in the eyes, touched two fingertips delicately to her forehead and, in turn, bowed gracefully to both me and Carter, and then turned with a rustle of black taffeta and stepped without pause into the darkness of the mirror and was gone.

Moran had heard the commotion, and with his patients sedated, he had come running up the stone steps to offer what help he could. He quickly surveyed the wreckage of the room and went at once to Makepeace who still lay on the floor, where shock had clouded his eyes. He bent down and helped him to his feet, slipped a bandage over the man's thin shoulders to form a makeshift sling for his broken arm.

Carter stood looking out of the window, took in the light of the dawn as the sun slowly broke over the canopy of the trees in the courtyard below. He was stroking his dark beard, pulling it through his fist into a point below his chin. He looked pale and tired but the first glimpse of a smile could be seen at the corners of his mouth. The sun rose over the city in the distance, illuminated the trees, the colors of fall glowed from their branches, copper and burgundy, portents of a glorious day, one at last filled with hope. The rain clouds from the night had finally dispersed and swallows swooped and danced, hunted for flies across the courtyard in the slowly warming air of the new day.

Edgar lay unmoving on the ground and I knelt beside him. A thin and reedy pulse still circulated what meagre blood he still contained. I rested his head in my lap. His limbs were thin and his cheeks were hollow, but slowly his eyelids opened to show a sliver of dark ebony. His face was clear and sane. His broad brow showed no sign of fever and at the last he was calm and clear in his thoughts.

"Joseph," he whispered, barely audible, his breath faint.

"I am here Edgar, I am here at last. I am so sorry I left you and took so long to return."

His eyes dimmed and his head fell slowly back, a weight in my lap.

"I am glad you returned. Finally…a surcease of sorrow."

I recognized the line from his poem, the Raven "Yes Edgar, you are freed at last. The demon has departed, you are free."

The rising sun, at last, tilted over the window-sill and bathed his tender, pale face in warm sunlight and reflected brightly from his pupils. Carter walked slowly across and knelt beside us and Moran and Makepeace shuffled to join us. I held his hand as he struggled for breath. What blood remained within him drained slowly from his face and I gripped his hand to reassure him that now, at the end he was not alone. A sound from the corridor outside startled us all to attention. Miraculously, the two brothers stood framed, indomitable  in the doorway. Volk's hands were bandaged but he held them, bent at the elbows, out in front of him like battering rams. Darko glowered from his empty eye sockets. He was blind, but his visage strongly suggested he was aware of the scene in front of him, his intent focused on Edgar's recumbent body.

A tear slipped from my eyes and rolled slowly down my check to fall at last onto the face of my dear friend. The journey had been arduous and the loss too great. A mysterious realm who's existence I would have scoffed at mere days before had been revealed to me and I was changed forever. I wished with all of my heart I could have seen the truth and helped him sooner. Carter reached across and touched my shoulder, a kind and simple gesture of friendship and reassurance. I looked up and met his gaze, no words were needed. I looked around at my friends, Carter, Moran and Makepeace, Volk and Darko. A curious group to be certain, but I would not have exchanged their being there with me for the world. We shared a quiet moment of introspection as we listened to Edgar's increasingly shallow breaths, almost soundless against the life and vitality of the bird song beyond the window. The birds embraced and noisily celebrated the touch of the new dawn and gave succor to our sadness and suffering.

Edgar's eyes fluttered closed and he sank further into my lap but he seemed to be aware of the songbirds and his head cocked to listen. A faint crooked smile touched his lips and his eyelids parted. He looked me directly in the eyes.

"God help my poor soul," he said at last. And then weakly, a whisper, "the fever called living I have conquered at last."

And with that he slipped away to continue his journey alone, freed at last from the demons, both physical and mental, that had haunted, tormented and pursued him. He left us, this curious group, to continue the quest. To retrace his earthly footsteps once more, to seek out those who would serve evil and meet it with absolute retribution and vengeance wherever it was to be found.

## *About the Author*

Originally from the United Kingdom, Andy has lived with his wife Paula and their two dogs Archie and Pi in Atlanta GA for the last fifteen years (with the exception of a year in Spain/UK during the pandemic). I love reading a good, heavy novel and enjoy Sci-Fi. At heart always British, I love life in the U.S.A but you will never hear me speak the American pronunciations of basil, banana or tomato.

Made in the USA
Columbia, SC
20 June 2021

39600956R00126